THE AMARIAND

Part - I

THE COVEN GATE

PRIYA SRINIVASAN

notionpress.com

INDIA • SINGAPORE • MALAYSIA

ISBN 979-8-88733-675-6

CONTENTS

INTRODUCTION

A future king from a small kingdom set out to shatter the disparities happening in the North Island. After going through failure, struggle, love, pain and revenge, he unites all the kingdoms of North Island and rule under his throne as, 'The Amariand'. This story happens in the late medieval period between two major islands, the North Island and the South Island. The story is told in three different parts: The beginning- 'THE COVEN GATE', the challenge- 'THE PERILOUS SNOWLAND', and the victory- 'THE DESCEND OF TWIN KINGDOM'.

CHAPTER 1

THE CORONATION

A grand ceremony was arranged for Prince Glartons' coronation. Ministers, friends, relatives, and the citizens have gathered in the embellished royal court. The kings of various provinces have gathered along with their family members. Prince Glarton was dressed in a most sophisticated and elegant robe. He was sitting majestically on the throne showing pride on his face. He turned to his right and graciously looked at his father, King Themton, and his siblings, Princess Athena and Prince Hadeton. Then he quirked a brief smile to his ministers and friends, who were sitting on his left.

King Themton got up from his seat and looked at his son with pride in his face. He advanced to the person who was holding a plate. On the plate was a velvety rich quality cushion cloth, which had a crown: the Crown of Emerald. King Themton sighted at the crown and glanced at his elder sister, Queen Pearly, who was standing adjacent to Princess Athena. He understood that she has many unanswered questions. When he touched the crown, it gave him a hair on end feeling. As the king lifted the crown from the plate; the light from the oil lamp chandelier and the rising sun rays fell on the crown. The beautiful emerald stone on the crown glowed enhancing the beauty of the crown.

King raised the crown high up and showed to the crowd who had gathered in the courtyard. The light reflection from the emerald glared the eyes of the crowd, and they felt mesmerized. The crowd shouted, "Hail for King Themton." As King Themton started walking towards Prince Glarton, the commander, ministers and priests stood up and bowed to the crown. There was silence in the hall and everyone was eagerly waiting to see the crown placed on Prince Glartons' head.

Every step King Themton was taking towards Prince Glarton, he felt the crown becoming heavier and heavier. King could not understand what was going on. He thought, is the crown really growing heavier with every step or is he becoming weak. Therefore, he was taking each and every step slowly. Glarton saw his father carrying the crown with lot of difficulty. He got worried that his father may fall down, but King Themton somehow managed to carry the crown to Glarton.

As king lifted the crown to place it on Glartons' head, it became heavier for him to lift it anymore. It slipped from King Themtons' hand and fell down on the ground making a huge 'dang' sound. Immediately the crown melted into a green emerald liquid, which converted to an acid, and vaporized and merged with the ground. The astonished king looked at Glarton, who also slowly melted and began to vanish. He screamed "Glarton!" and ran towards him. Unfortunately, before he could near him, Glarton completely vanished away.

Themton gazed around: Princess Athena, Prince Hadeton, ministers and everyone else were gradually vanishing. Only his sister, Queen Pearly was standing next to the throne. There was vibration on the floor causing the throne, chandelier, wall lamps, and portraits to fall down. A huge crack appeared on the floor and it grew wider creating a hole. The earth began to engulf the things and Queen Pearly as well. Themton wanted to save her; however, he could not move his legs. Queen Pearly looked at him for the last time and screamed, "No Themton! No! Do not do this. Do not go against the truth, which is more powerful."

King Themton awoke startled from his sleep. He opened his eyes and looked around him. His face was sweating and his lungs were gasping for air. He realized that he was on his bed and had a nightmare. The early morning sunrise illuminated the room. King Themton went to the end of the room, where there was a thick bowl containing water. He wiped the sweat and washed his face with water. He could see his reflection in the water.

The reflection changed to Queen Pearlys' face, who was staring at him in anger. He became agitated, and did not want to see the angry face of his sister. He vigorously shook the bowl to make the image disappear. Inspite of vigor, he could still see the image of his sisters' face. It created irritation for King Themton. Not able to control this aggravation, he punched the bowl and it broke into pieces. The sharp edges tore the skin of his fingers. He wiped off the blood from his hand and stared at the broken pieces. He uttered with pain, "Pearly, my integrity is stronger than the truth."

CHAPTER 2

18-YEAR-OLD PRINCE

Through the window of his bedchamber, King Themton could see his Kingdom, Azunt getting adorned to celebrate the eighteenth birth anniversary of Prince Glarton. In the land of Azunt a custom was followed: every year on the birth date of members of royal families, saplings were planted along the borders of the palace. The number of saplings planted are same as the age of the royals. Accordingly, today servants were planting 18 young plants. Because of this custom, the palace was always surrounded by flourishing green plants and trees, colorful fruits and nice aromatic flowers. Drawn towards these there were many varieties of butterflies, birds and small domestic animals.

Azunt was the smallest kingdom in the North Island. It was protected on all sides by tall fort. The west part was covered by the river thus, "Hoo….Ssh"! sound created by the waves always echoed on the wall that was facing the shore. In the North Island, the palace for the royal family was located inside the fort. In Azunt, the palace was located at the west end of the fort, whereas the citizens lived along with agricultural lands in the east and the rest covered by lakes and ponds.

The palace had an arch shaped entrance with huge and strong pillars on either side. These pillars were bearing beautiful sculpture of ladies in a welcoming pose. From outside, the palace looked small whereas inside it is huge. In the courtyard, the high dome shaped roof with multiple glasses were providing illumination. Moreover, the tall ceiling reduced the heat by giving natural ventilation for the palace. There were special stained-glass windows in the bedchambers. The roof in the feast hall had provisions for opening and closing.

Inside the palace, Prince Glarton was readying himself with expensive robes and ornaments for this significant day. His upward combed brown color hair gently ended on his shoulder and nape. His face: some may say its oval or almost round, had broad forehead. He had very sharp brown eyes with thick eyebrows. Following the eyes laid a distinct nose, visible philtrum, small thin lips, and a rounded chin. Whenever he spoke, his well-defined lower jaw line moved elegantly.

A male servant entered Prince Glartons' room, bowed to him and mentioned that his Majesty is expecting his Highness presence in the Feast room. The prince smiled and gestured that he shall be arriving soon. He left his room and entered a passage, where his four childhood friends were waiting for him. These childhood friends are also the kings of various territories of Azunt. They wished Glarton for long life and all of them entered an illuminated huge Feast room.

The center ceiling of the hall was holding a huge and beautiful oil lamp chandelier. The walls of the room had beautiful portraits of King Themton, and his family members. As Glarton entered the room, those who were gathered in the hall stood up. There were noises of happiness. Glartons' siblings, Princess Athena and Prince Hadeton were twins. They were two years younger. They ran to Glarton, hugged and wished him. After hugging his siblings, Glarton walked towards his father, King Themton; who hugged and wished a long life for him.

Those who were seeing Prince Glarton after many years were amazed by his towered six feet and above tall stature, handsome looks, and well-built shoulders. King Themton was full of pride to see his eighteen-year-old son being admired by the guests. Anyone who sees the King might understand from whom Prince Glarton got his majestic looks. In the courtyard, when King Themton rested on his throne and glanced around, everybody can sense an air of magnificence. His Majesty was forty-three-year-old tall, well-built, and has greyish black hair. Because of years of wisdom, his brown eyes were calm and matured. The glory that radiates from the face of King Themton made others bow to him with respect.

The feast hall had a long refectory table at the center, which was filled with three types of wines, variety of fruits, and four huge plates of meats. Moreover, there were bread, corn and peas, with sweet relishes. Around this table there were many small tables and chairs for guest to sit and enjoy the food. In one corner, there were musicians playing on various musical instruments such as oud, slit drum, harp, flute, and clappers.

Due to the occasion: different types of horses, beautifully embellished chariots and male servants of the guests were standing outside the palace. The sun was setting gradually and the servants of the palace lit the fuel lamps on the wall, candles in the middle of the tables, and the huge oil lantern lamps hanging on the corner of the ceiling. Under the full moon light, the illuminated palace with shore on its rear appeared marvelous.

Once all the important guests have arrived, King Themton arose from his chair and in his loud thunder voice said, "Today, my son, Prince Glarton turns eighteen. I welcome the satraps, rulers, families, and friends." Saying this he looked at the crowd and smiled.

He continued, "As a boy grows up, there are certain changes occurring at different age. At eight years, he understands his parents love for him, by twelve he shall be attracted to person of opposite sex, at fifteen he understands the implications he has towards his society, and when he turns eighteen years, he decides to choose a path for his desired future. I am glad to say that my son has come to a point in his life to choose his path to fulfill his destiny."

King raised his wine glass and toasted, "I thank all of you for being here. Long live Prince Glarton." Everybody in the feast hall raised glass of wine and responded by saying, "Long live prince Glarton. Long live King Themton." Everybody drank wine.

The ceremony was going well. Some were dancing, some were playing music, some were drinking unlimited wine, and the rest filling their stomach with delicious food. Everyone was happy and enjoying the gathering. It was becoming late night and the guests started leaving in their horses and chariots. The Lord and his family members remained seated in the center of the feast hall.

King Themton handed to his son a long plate, which had a gift covered in a velvet cloth. Prince Glarton uncovered it and found a double-edged sword. His eyes widened in surprise. He took the sword out of the scabbard. It was a beautiful sword with a star shaped carving on the hilt. The center of the carving had a small green emerald stone. Using his left hand, he swung it gently and the sword moved elegantly with ease. When he was admiring the sword for its length, the balance at the hilt, and the sharp edges; the light from the huge chandelier reflected on the sword. The glow on Glartons' face showed his adoration towards the sword.

He placed the sword back in its scabbard; then hugged his father and said, "I thank you father."

King Themton nodded his head and spoke, "My son, you have turned eighteen. Your destiny is to become the king and take care of our kingdom and its people. What is your next step towards that?"

"Father, I am glad you asked. I wanted to ask you something since few days, but ...," Glarton hesitated.

"What is it Glarton?" King signed Glarton to sit next to him and continued, "I have always treated you like a future King. Hence, ask without difficulty."

"Father, I wish to go to Coven."

"Coven?"

With slight hesitation Prince Glarton answered, "Yes... father."

"For what?"

Prince Glarton answered, "I have heard a lot about Sir Urases, his teachings and especial training he provides in Coven. I hope to go there and learn from him."

King Themton glanced at Prince Hadeton and Princess Athena, and after a pause he asked, "Go out of your kingdom for training? Do you know, it takes many years to finish the training provided by Sir Urases?"

"Yes, I do. I did not get the strength to ask you, because I know you shall not be happy if I am far from home for many years."

"Not able to see you for 3 to 5 years!" The King gazed away from his three children and took a deep breath. He turned to Glarton and continued, "We will yearn for your return."

Prince Glarton requested, "Father...may I take your leave?"

"Glarton, in our dynasty, all Princes got trained inside our Kingdom. May I ask why you are certain in receiving more training at Coven?"

"Since childhood, I have this wish to unite all the kingdoms in the North Island and reign under one throne."

King was little surprised to hear this. After a pause he asked, "What?"

"Father, to bring an entire Island under one throne… one emperor; a wish since I was twelve. To achieve this, I need to acquire knowledge and hone more skills. Sir Urases is respected as the best teacher."

Immediately, King Themton gave a hopeless smile. Prince Glarton got worried, "Did I say anything wrong or you feel I am having an impossible goal."

"No! Glarton, no. Once, I aspired the same. Although, I could not pursue the wish. Seldom, it still burns as a flame in my thoughts."

"May I ask what happened?"

King wanted to reply, but the thought of his past incidents made his body shiver. He relaxed his body and managed by saying, "It is a long story…A… long story…" He exhaled heavily and continued, "I am glad you are pursuing my dream. Go ahead."

"I thank you," said Glarton happily.

"Always believe in you. You will achieve it and I have no uncertainty in that. You have chosen the right place to receive your training. When do you have to go?" asked King.

"As soon as possible," replied Prince.

"Sir Urases is a great teacher. At once, I will send a request message to him and also, to Camigo. Glarton, hope you remember Camigo; my old friend, he lives in Coven."

Prince Glarton said, "Yes, I remember. Father, your support and love are great blessings for me."

Father and son hugged each other. Glarton was joyful about this journey and the training. Unfortunately, he did not know that this journey is going to become an unforgettable incident in his life.

CHAPTER 3

THE FIVE TERRITORIES

There were two major islands: the North Island and the South Island. There were five major kingdoms in the North Island namely, Samb, Omiw, Azunt, Goptm and Nosoe. The interesting facts about these kingdoms were that each had unique language, culture, and traditions. They had their own flag, which was diagonally divided by a red line.

For generations, the king of each kingdom wore a ring which served as their emblem. The courtyard had an experienced Master whose main role was to teach the children of the royal family. Furthermore, they provided guidance to the King when needed. These Masters were competent in the language of their neighboring kingdoms; therefore, when needed, they acted as a translator.

Samb was located on the northern region of the North Island. The neighbors were: Beringia in the North, Omiw in the South, and Nosoe in the East and South

East. The western part of Samb was entirely surrounded by sea. Beringia was a huge snow-covered mountain area believed to be inhabited by ferocious animals. The upper part of the flag had image of fish, dog sleigh and the lower part had Mount Beringia. Its' emblem was moon. Samb was ruled by King Amgosh. He was so obsessed with wealth and power, which he disliked to share with anyone. Hence, he neither wished to marry nor wanted to have a heir.

Year around it was cold or snowy; therefore, Sambans wore layers of dresses, thick heavy shoes and headgear. Being mostly an icy land, the main mode of transportation was through dog sleighs. People mainly relied on fishing, and hunting animals for food. Because of strong freezing weather, the Sambans were not much active, and sluggish in nature yet, they were ferocious and aggressive. Most part of the day, people were seen drunk with wine. Their food mainly comprised of seafood, salted meat, syrup, stew, quinoa, and flax.

Omiw was located in the north-west region of the North Island. It shared borders with Samb in North, Azunt in South, Nosoe in East and enclosed by water in the West. As the northern part had mostly cold weather and the southern part mostly warm, Omiw experienced a mixed temperature. The upper part of the flag had an image of rising sun on a snow-covered mountain, and the lower part had cow and chicken. The Emblem was a circle with one side having half of a bull face and another half of a fish face.

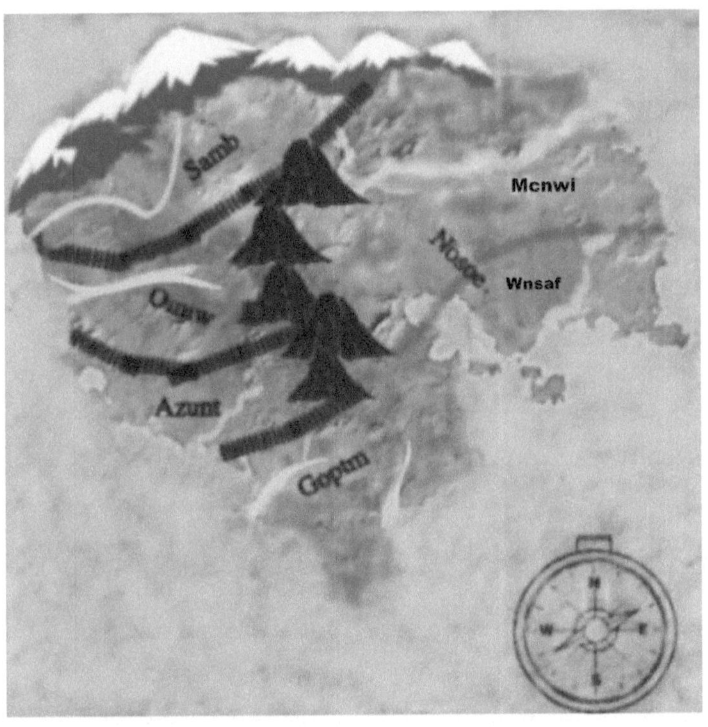
Samb
Mcnwi
Nbsae
Wnsaf
Onpw
Azunt
Goptm

Omiw was ruled by King Ercle: a very kind, generous and sympathetic person, due to which several people around him were taking advantage. Omiwans relied on agriculture and fishing. They were conservative and contended with their own territory. It had numerous provinces with minimum population, where people lived like a close-knit community. Food mainly comprised of sweet onion, potato, berries, hazelnuts and seafood.

Azunt was a small kingdom in the North Island. Its' neighbors were: Omiw in the North, Goptm in the South, Nosoe in the East and enclosed by sea in the West. It was ruled by King Themton. After the death of his wife Queen Heran, along with the kingdom he took care of his family. People mainly relied on agriculture and were culturally rich. The main entertainment was theater, where they performed singing, dancing and enacting the literature or tradition.

Being the smallest territory, Azuntans were simple and contended with what they had. The upper part of the flag had an image of wheat and corn and the lower part had an image of a man and a woman dancing. The emblem was sun. Year around the weather was warm to hot, with few cold days, hence they wore small and thin clothes. They mostly had rice, almonds, beets, and cherries.

Goptm is located in the southern part of the North Island. It was surrounded in North West by Azunt and in North East by Nosoe and the rest by water. King Ndorms ruled Goptm with benevolence, for which

Goptmans adored him. The upper part of the flag had an image of wooden plough and the lower part had rice and corn. The emblem was corn knife. Half of the year was rainy and the rest was mostly warm to hot. Since it is surrounded mostly by water, people relied on fishing and the rain helped them to harvest agriculture. Goptmans were highly traditional and gave importance to family and culture. Largely they consumed: rice, corn, beans and seafood. People wore thin layered clothes and loved ornaments. Men and women wore accessories made of seashells.

The biggest and most powerful kingdom in the North Island was Nosoe. It almost covered the entire left half of the North Island. Its neighbors were: Samb and Beringia Mountain in the North, Goptm in the South, Omiw and Azunt in the West and sea in the East. Nosoe had rainy, snowy and hot climates. The crown was the emblem. Nosoe was ruled by King Ialkrit: the strongest and the most ferocious. Poets admired him as ruling with an iron fist. He was popular for his highly trained Imperial fighters. The upper part of the flag had an image of two crossed swords and the lower part had gold.

During the reign by King Ialkrit the huge land was divided into North Mcnwi and South Wnsaf. Mcnwi was ruled by King Ialkrit, and Wnsaf by his younger brother King Juakrit, who was popular for his righteousness and spirituality. Mcnwi was mostly rainy and snowy whereas Wnsaf had mostly warm to hot weather. Hence the people of Nosoe traveled between Mcnwi and Wnsaf to enjoy the different temperatures.

In Mcnwi the food mainly comprised of corn, pumpkins, apples, tomatoes, and cranberries. In Wnsaf it was spinach, peanuts, peppers, sweet potatoes, and oranges. Nosoe had well established trading and transport system. Being the powerful and prosperous dynasty, people had lot of pride, which resulted in insulting traders and visitors coming from other kingdoms.

The Giant Mountains had a great significance in the North Island. It was a range of mountains of different proportions, which seemed to be intermittent. It ran from the North, the border of Samb to the South, the border of Goptm, majorly dividing Nosoe from Omiw and Azunt. These mountain ranges served as a big barrier protecting Omiw and Azunt, and providing monsoon rains. Several of these mountains were utilized for cultivations.

The intermountain valleys were deep and mysterious, mostly covered by thick forests. Some of these valleys were used as a passage for transportation between Eastern and Western regions. Unfortunately, these valleys were abused by highwaymen to attack travelers and traders passing through the valleys. King Ialkrit strongly forbade trading with any neighboring kingdoms; wherefore several traders utilized these valleys for secret trading between the territories. It was revealed that the regional satraps around these valleys had secret tunnels, which were used for spying.

Ages ago a story stated -- there was a narrow passage connecting the North and the South Islands. It connected the Cape of Goptm (North Island) to the Coven Gate (South Island). This passage helped many people to earn money by selling merchandise between Goptm and Coven. One day, it suddenly got drowned by the water. A local folk story explains the reason for this sudden disappearance of the passage.

CHAPTER 4

MY DEAR SON

On the night of Prince Glartons' birth anniversary, King Themton was walking in his bedchamber corridor. The vision that he had for ages is going to become real because of his son still, he grew restless when the incidents from the past tried to haunt him. Glartons' mother Queen Heran, his first love…, marriage…, and the humiliation; thoughts flowing like unstoppable stream. This flow of thought was ended with the Nosoe incident, the irreparable ruin.

King Themton does not want to think anything further. He went near his bed and viewed the portrait of his children on the wall. The thoughts gradually changed to a pleasant one. Queen Heran died when Prince Glarton was five years old. Since childhood Prince Glarton has proved being an honest and a brave boy. When Glarton was fourteen, the Master took him along with other children to the vast ground near the border of Azunt. The Master was training them in fencing.

At the border, Glarton saw small huts on the North side whereas large homes on the East side. There were differences in the people's clothing and living conditions. People in the huts were living penniless life and he could hear few children weeping because of hunger. When the Master was teaching, he inquired about the huts and their condition. The Master explained the disparities between the kingdoms and the decrees by the strong dynasty.

Glarton could not accept and started debating with the Master, who were not able to make him understand. Glarton was agitated and showed it while practicing with the sword. The Master saw his strong moves and ordered him to calm down. Glarton continued his vigorous moves and defeated all other children. The Master informed the king about the incident. He also added that his Highness has a good vision with respect to the future, unfortunately, it may not be achievable. The present situation is making Glarton unhappy. He wishes to remove the decrees creating discrimination and hatred among the people of different kingdoms.

King Themton thoughts now went to the future of Azunt. It is wonderful to see a future, wherein all the territories are united impartial to: superior or inferior, large or small, rich or poor, strong or weak. At present, Azunt is growing weaker; Prince Glarton must become a mighty king and make it happen. What if he is not able to do? Revenge...! Will Glarton be able to take revenge? All these questions were troubling king Themton.

As he was thinking about the past, he remembered an unforgettable person, Camigo; a good old friend, and an interesting character. On the way back to Azunt, Themton met Camigo at the border near Mcnwi. He was fully heartbroken; it was Camigo who comforted him and encouraged him. Camigo was talented; spoke multiple languages, and always eager to explore the forest. They were in contact, until the day King Themton got the last message from Camigo.

Camigo was threatened by King Ialkrit. He was scared, and his own people accused him of being a betrayer to his own king. His everyday life was becoming bad. Hence, unwillingly Camigo left the North Island, and went to the South Island. After a decade, King Themton got a message from Camigo stating that he has shifted to Coven and began a new life. In addition, in his message, he has referred highly about Coven.

King Themton gave a relaxed smile, trusting his son will be in good hands. Next day morning King Themton sent a message to Camigo.

"Dear old friend Camigo,
Warm Greetings. Hope you are in good health. It has been years since we have personally met. Neither the distance nor the years can stop me from remembering you. My son, Prince Glarton has turned eighteen and intend to receive training from Sir Urases. He might

reach Coven in the following days. Herewith, I am sending his portrait. In your last message, you have mentioned the hurdles and restrictions of entering Coven, which I have not informed Glarton. I feel his training and learning starts the moment he departs this province. Kindly meet him only after you have been sent a word by a particular person from the Coven Gate. My friend kindly note, I desire you to help him only when there is a true emergency. My son should survive and prove himself as an individual and not as a Prince of Azunt. I am certain that you will take care of him as family.

Your friend,
Themton. ”

Inspite of knowing the curse, and the hardships in entering Coven through the Coven Gate, Themton did not inform anything to Prince Glarton. He wanted his son to experience and survive all by himself. He did not make any special arrangements for his journey or stay. Prince Glarton understood his fathers' intention that he has to gain confidence through his own experience and thus, he did not ask his father for anything.

After two days, Prince Glarton was ready to begin his journey. He carried the sword presented by his father along with a portrait of his father and siblings. At the forepart of the palace, royal family members and citizens gathered. Prince Glarton bowed to his father and King Themton embraced him. As he hugged him, his heart grew heavier with the thought of separation for next several years. He comforted his heart knowing many provinces shall prosper by this.

King Themton said, "My blessings are always with you, my son. And do not forget; your mother is looking and guiding you from heaven."

"I thank you father."

Citizens shouted, "Long live Prince Glarton, long live King Themton."

Prince Glartons' friends insisted on accompanying him till the end of the North Island. Glarton and his friends mounted on their horse and rode off. Glarton looked back to his father, younger sister Princess Athena and younger brother Prince Hadeton. With tear laden eyes, he lifted his hand gesturing for good journey. As they were riding, sand smokes were filling the place and after few moments it disappeared among the dusts. Citizens and royal member dispersed, but King Themton was standing at the same place. Princess Athena went near him, held his hand, and took him inside the palace.

In the following days King Themton looked sorrowful, and this worried the ministers and others in the courtyard. The ministers tried to comfort the king; however, they failed. Princess Athena and Prince Hadeton came to meet him at Kings' chamber. Athena knew how much Themton loved her brother. She tried to comfort him by saying, "Father, I have never seen you worried like this. I understand your pain but seeing you sad makes us sad. For our happiness, do not worry."

Prince Hadeton comforted by saying, "Father, you know about brother Glarton. Do not worry! He will be fine."

"My children, I am aware Glarton is a brave boy. However, at present, I am not. Still, your words provide solace."

Princess urged, "Father, I also wish to go to a faraway land for a long time."

"Why dear?"

"Thenceforth, you will talk more about me. In past two days you have admired about Glarton to almost everyone in this palace!"

King Themton laughed aloud, "Dear princess, I have the same love for all three of you. If one of you go far away, for a long time, I will be yearning the same." Hearing this Athena embraced her father.

Hadeton said, "Father, I am eagerly waiting to go for my special training at Coven. Once brother returns, I will be glad to go."

"Ho! No, no… my dear youngest son. Your brother is my life and you are my heart. Furthermore, you are too soft for this special training. Let your brother do those, you shall always be near me as my little son."

King Themton caressed Athenas' head and asked, "If you can go outside this kingdom where would you wish to go?"

Athena replied without delay, "Nosoe."

"What? I mean for what?"

"Since I was a little girl, I have heard great stories about the beauty of Nosoe. Frequently, I have listened from our Master: the magnificent palace, the abundance, the great warriors and more." King Themton listened to her quietly.

Athena continued, "In addition, in the past few years, I have heard words on the wonderful art work of the twin kingdom. If I can go… I shall happily go to Nosoe and admire its natural beauty." King Themton was not happy to hear this and wished she never goes there. Nevertheless, he cannot restrict her from knowing her family. Therefore, he did not reply anything, and kept smiling.

CHAPTER 5

COVEN AND THE COVEN GATE

Coven is located in the Northern part of the South Island. It is a land of greenery, as though the green paint was accidentally spilled over Coven. There were many varieties of flowers in different colors, adding beauty to the greenery. Small waterfalls at all the corners of Coven were enhancing the appeal. These waterfalls created many small ponds in between the lands, which were beautifying Coven similar to an accessory on the face of a beautiful girl. It had volcanoes, but they were also only adding value. While creating Coven, the creator would have been in an artistic mood.

Coven is reasonably a big kingdom surrounded by water in the North, East, and West and by Brozin territory in the South. It had rich fertile soil. People mostly relied on fishing and agriculture. Their food mainly comprised of seafood, rice, bananas, and coconuts. Year around it experiences warm to hot weather. Frequently, it had days which were neither hot nor cold, similar to the nature of the people of Coven, who were neither soft nor rough. The houses were well planned and arranged in line with the same pattern.

There were two major communities in Coven. The North-East region had Zeulean community, and the South-West region had Lumbian community. These two regions were majorly separated by Mount Agua. Both communities had almost the same culture, language and tradition. Each community had two community elders: Community Man and Community Woman. They were like the king and Queen of the community. Whenever there was any problem in the community, citizens approached the community elders.

Additionally, each community had a prominent person, who was accepted as a leader. While solving problems, if needed, the Community Man and Woman got recommendations from the prominent person. For Zeulean, Mother Maurea was considered as the prominent person. The Zeuleans were protecting the north end of the South Island from any attack through the sea route. They had efficient sea route fighting system; well-built ships, weapons, archers carrying boats and people specially trained to combat under the water.

Both community people encouraged outside merchants to enter Coven with merchandise and do trading. This took place primarily through sea route. In the beginning, these trading were bringing new varieties of commodities and attracted extra wealth in to Coven.

However, over time, these trading resulted in various problems.

The Covenans had many bad experiences because of some traders who were highly cunning. They were selling poor quality products and taking advantage. At one point, Covenans were buying more goods from the outside traders than from the local merchants, which resulted in massive loss. It was not only the traders but also the visitors and scholars, who came from outside were creating problems. Often, expensive things were stolen, occasionally men were killed and seldom women were kidnapped.

One fine day, the Community Man and the Community Woman of both Zeulean and Lumbian communities, along with the prominent person of the community, gathered to discuss a solution. They imposed a rule, which stated that any foreigners who entered Coven: for trading or training or for a short journey or for settling down has to be thoroughly verified.

The Coven Gate was the primary port of entry into Coven. It had two tall and strong stone pillars on either side, with an arch connecting them. These pillars were bearing two huge wooden doors which had a heavy iron latch on the inside. A thick stone fence from the sides of these pillar extended and covered the Coven border. As the entire fence was guarded, people coming to Coven by sea route or land had to enter only through this Coven Gate. Anybody who tried to enter by a different route would be punished by the guard. Even if the guard miss them, the venomous creatures which were grown intentionally around the fence may kill them.

A small group of people stayed at the Coven Gate; who were engaged in securing the entry and was overseen by Mother Maurea. There was a vast land adjacent to the Gate which had properly maintained huts. The huts designated for staying (for both the workers and newcomers) had all basic and similar facilities. Mother Maurea hut was located in the center of all the huts.

People entering Coven from other territories were treated the same, irrespective of their custom, tradition or earning. Those who entered the Gate have to stay in the hut for three days and undergo scrutiny conducted by Maurea and her group. They should prove that they were good, honest and not harmful. Sometimes having special qualities helped them to get in. Only those who succeeded were allowed to enter Coven. Whereas the rest were given a permanent red colored dot on the inner side of the left hand adjacent to the wrist, which prevented them from re-entering into Coven. People possessing the red dot try to enter by bribes were severely punished till death and thrown into the sea.

At the Coven Gate, Maurea employed many men and women, whose work was to examine the newcomers entering the Coven Gate. She has trained them to observe and find various nefarious activities. Seldom thieves or spies from neighboring territories entered Coven. Through the various methods Mother Maurea and her group were able to segregate or identify the good from the bad and proceed. According to the purpose of the journey, the strangers were questioned. If the newcomer was a trader, they were inquired regarding the commodities, previous experience, and their plan to handle the hurdles in a new place.

If the person was suspected as a thief or a spy, decision was made by examining their belongings, and indirectly creating opportunities for them to steal. The procedure took few days, until then they have to stay in the hut. During the stay, they have to help the workers of the hut in agriculture, cleaning, cooking, and washing.

CHAPTER 6

MOTHER MAUREA

Mother Maurea, aged about ninty years, was a tall and medium built woman who was born and brought up in a small town adjacent to the Coven Gate. The wrinkles on her forehead spoke of her wisdom and the full white hair of her head revealed the years of experience she had. The thick scaly skin of her body showed the years of problems she has faced, and her mild hunchback was because of giving her energy to help those in need.

Few people at Coven believed that her father was a great Master who got wisdom directly from the higher spirits and her mother was a person possessing exceptional healing power. Over the years, the Covenans kept passing the story regarding the power and wisdom of Maurea to their children, who in turn continued it to the next generation. The elders at Coven stated that she was born to a woman named Arinin, the person who was responsible for the immersion of the isthmus, a narrow strip of land connecting the North and the South Island.

Some 100 years back, in a small town at the Cape of Goptm in the North Island, lived a girl named Arinin. When she was young, her parents comprehended her capacity to heal any kind of ailments. Initially, they were hesitant but when people of the town found out, they became comfortable and admired her powers. When she turned twenty, she involved herself absolutely in helping those in health-related needs, by using her natural powers. The people of the town cherished her services and respected her for her noble deeds. She was respected as a holy spirit who was guarding the entire town.

One day, two traders from the South Island came to Cape of Goptm for the purpose of trading. They heard about Arinin and were curious to meet her. Pretending to be sick, they met her. On the first meeting, they were spell bound by her beauty. Arinin was a simple girl, although her face had richness of beauty. Both men could not take their eyes off her face. They were melting away with her talk, expressions and body language.

For the next few days, they kept meeting her often, for invalid reasons. Arinin and her parents were not comfortable. So, one day, when they showed up at the entrance, Arinins' father stopped and warned them. Both men conveyed their wish to marry her; the one she chooses will marry her and the other help them in their marriage. Arinin and her parents were startled on hearing this and felt bad.

Her father decided to call the local leader, but Arinin stopped him. In a calm, yet stern voice Arinin explained to the traders that it is impossible for her to marry. Adding on, she said that since childhood she wanted to only serve people and will continue to do so forever. The two men were not ready to accept this, and kept persuading. For many days she was troubled. Seeing the men often near Arinins' home and her parents' reactions, the town people understood what was going on. People grew furious; they beat the traders badly, insulted them by throwing cow dung on the face and kicked them out of the town.

The men ran away from the town and hid in a place on the passage that was connecting the North and the South Island. They planned their revenge in humiliation. One night, when the whole town was sleeping, they kidnapped Arinin. They brought her to the isthmus where they were hiding and violated her. She became insensible, so the traders left her at the cape tip and escaped through the isthmus to their hometown in the South Island. It was remarked that after regaining health, Arinin cursed the traders. She also cursed the passage because it paved a way for the traders to hide, attack and escape.

Gradually, the water level surrounding the isthmus raised high and flowed over the land and engulfed it in the manner of a starving crocodile. In a short period, the two traders lost their good looks and roamed around like beggars in Coven. In the end what happened to them, no one precisely knew. Rumors stated, after the locals of Coven ascertained the unbearable sin the two traders had committed; they created a huge fire and threw them alive into the fire.

The isthmus has helped in trading between Goptm and Coven and for easy riding between the North and South Island. So, prominent persons from Goptm and the locals requested Arinin to help them. Respecting the request, Arinin predicted, "A period shall come in the future, when the son of the Great King from the North Island cross this land and go to the South Island, will revolt against the cruel reign of the king, defeat him and conquer the South Island. Blood of his true spirit, shed on this land, shall remove the curse. Thenceforth, rise a narrow land from beneath the water, which will again connect the two Islands."

Due to the bad incident, Arinin was pregnant. Initially, she hid it from her parents and neighbors; however, in due course she could no longer hide her pregnancy. The residents could not accept this. They took this as a bad sign and strongly believed it could bring darkness to the town. So, many suggested her to kill the baby in its womb, which she refused. As she has taken care of the residents, they did not compel her. At the border of Goptm adjacent to the river, they built a small hut and pleaded her to spend the rest of her life there.

Everyday food was delivered to her house and once in a while a mid-wife attended her. Even though being taken care, Arinin was sad because she could not lead a normal life. During the ninth month of pregnancy, she intuited of having difficulties in giving birth. If anything, worse happens, she was scared that the child may not be treated properly in Goptm. Therefore, she planned to leave the place and sail to Nosoe, which was the nearby land. Few loyal supporters helped her obtain a canoe. They filled the boat with necessary food and clothes for Arinin and the two sailors.

One day, before the dawn, they secretly sailed out of Goptm. As the two sailors were sailing the canoe for a while, from nowhere thick clouds surrounded the sky. Unfortunately, heavy rain progressed to thunder storm causing strong swaying of the canoe. The sailors could not control its motion and the canoe hit on a submerged rock. The canoe broke and all of them fell in to the water. The strong water currents took away the sailors and Arinin was struggling to swim carrying a living human in her womb.

Because of her struggle against the strong water currents, Arinin got into pain. She had no choice except to deliver the baby under the water. Holding the new born life in one hand, she kept swimming using the other hand. Sadly, with each movement she became weaker, and she could no longer hold the baby and swim. She spotted a flat piece of wood floating on the water. She reached for it and placed the baby on the wood piece.

In a distance she saw a land. As she almost reached the shore, a huge wave dragged her fiercely. She knew this is her last possibility to save the baby. Hence, using all her strength she pushed the wood towards the shore. The wooden shaft swept on the shore sands and the baby landed safely on the soft muddy shore. The huge wave pulled Arinin away, as if it was telling that her work is done, and it is time for her to go.

She could see someone in the land running towards the baby on the shore. When she was about to lift her hand for help, the wave stopped her and took her with it. She never knew that she dropped the baby in the same land which she hated. The baby landed on Coven, South Island and was taken up by a fisherman who named her Maurea.

Because of her mother, Maurea acquired innate powers through which she can heal the illness of the health. In addition, she can foretell the future to an extent which has helped Covenans. The older generations of Coven were much aware of the power of Mother Maurea. They believed and respected her for her wisdom and powers. They had no doubts regarding the people, whom she chooses to enter Coven.

CHAPTER 7

A BEAUTIFUL LAND

Glarton was joyful to go to the new land and get trained from one of the great teachers. Glartons' four childhood friends accompanied him till the Cape of Goptm, which was located at the south tip of Goptm. On a bright day with clear sky, from this Cape, one can see a small part of Coven of the South Island. For those passing through the Goptm to the Cape of Goptm, there was a path through the west coast, which was most commonly used. Glarton and his friends came through this path. From Azunt, riding on horseback, it took three days for them to reach the Cape.

On the first night, after they left Azunt, they stayed at the border of Azunt and Goptm. They spent the second night on the west coast of Goptm and the third night they rested at the Cape. During these three days of journey, Glarton had a feeling of someone following them, although he was uncertain. When he told this to his friends, they declined saying, since he is out of Azunt for the first time, he thinks like that. On the fourth morning, at the Cape, the friends said their farewells to Glarton and waited till he got on a boat. Once he was out of the view, they mounted back to Azunt.

The boat was specifically made to pick up travelers from Cape to Coven. It was a huge sailboat named, Theoi Halioi, meaning sea god in the native language of Coven. Everyday Theoi Halioi sailed only twice to and from Goptm: once in the morning and once in the evening. It was crescent shaped, ending in pointed tips at the bow and stern. The outer hull planks were carvel built. It was propelled by both sail and oar. The center of the deck had an oval shaped door leading to cabins; with few having provisions to lie down. Those occupying these cabins were members of royal family or rich merchants or preeminent persons.

Glarton was standing in the corner of the deck near the bow of the boat. The river seemed calm and beautiful. Every now and then a smooth wave came and touched the boat. The two sailors on either end guiding the navigation, and the four rowers who were propelling the boat were hymning a song.

"Look around

Look around

Here we come

Look around

Theoi Halioi on the waves

Heoi baoi goes our days."

At half way, Coven Gate was clearly visible. Glarton gazed back and front to see the border of both the North and the South Islands. As the boat was approaching Coven, alike Glarton, other passengers were also amazed by seeing the beauty of the land. The boat reached the staithe and one by one the people got down and walked on the quay.

At the entrance of the Coven Gate there were guards, who were stopping each and every passenger and asking their whereabouts. When it was Glartons' turn, a guard stopped him and enquired. Glarton replied his name, and mentioned that he has come from Azunt. Furthermore, he informed that he has come to receive training from Sir Urases. The guard was familiar with Azunt, and observing Glartons' dress and accessories, he got a doubt; thus, he contacted his chief.

The Chief was a short and well-built man with a bald head. He stood opposite to Glarton and studied him. With his dress and appearance, the Chief suspected that Glarton could be from a royal family. The Chief queried, "Are you a trader?"

"No, I am not," replied Glarton

"What is the purpose of your journey?"

"I am here to get trained from Sir Urases."

"Do you belong to any royal family?"

"Yes Chief, I am the prince of Azunt." The Chief took him to Mother Maurea.

They entered Mother Maureas' hut. There was a good aroma inside, which was giving a calm and spiritual sense. Mother Maurea was standing beside the window. She was looking outside at men who were working.

Maurea said, "Salutations Prince. Welcome to Coven." Without turning, she continued, "Your name?"

Glarton bowed and said, "Salutations Mother Maurea." He raised and continued, "I thank you for letting me in. My name is Glarton, son of King Themton; coming from Azunt, located above Goptm."

"I have heard about King Themton. Are you his only son?"

Glarton replied, "No. I have twin siblings: one sister, Princess Athena and one brother, Prince Hadeton."

"What makes you come to the South Island?"

"I have heard greatly about the teachings of Sir Urases. I have come here to learn from him." As he was talking, Maurea was reading his eyes and was making her own calculations. When Glarton was in the boat from Goptm to Coven, he gave attention to several passengers talking about Mother Maurea. He realized whatever the people in the boat spoke about her is real. She does have the power in her eyes, which was testing Glartons' honesty.

"Do you happen to know anybody here?" asked Mother.

Glarton thought for a minute and recalled, "Yes. My fathers' friend, uncle Camigo. He lives in the northern part of Coven. I have met him once."

Mother was not fully satisfied with this information. Usually, when a member of a royal family comes to Coven Gate, a message will be sent prior to inform Mother

Maurea. Sometimes, the person will be accompanied by few guards until entering Coven. Neither of this happened with Glarton. She knew Camigo; she has met him when he entered Coven and it was him who spoke about King Themton. She ordered the Chief to make arrangements for Glartons' stay. The Chief and Glarton bowed to Maurea and left the hut. Same day Maurea sent a message to Camigo.

Next morning, Glarton was woken up by the sunrays which entered the hut without any permission. He came out of the hut, and saw the pleasant sunrise. He walked to the Coven Gate and more or less able to see the land of Goptm. A pleasant breeze touched his face. Coven was beautiful with natures' work. On his left was a vast river running on its own way and wish. On his right, above the sea level, was the rising sun like a fire ball on the sky.

Glarton was becoming one with the nature. The rising red color sun, the white color sea shore, many tall green trees, and the pure smell of the sand were giving a wonderful feeling. Glarton wished to return to this place again along with his family and friends. Unfortunately, he did not know that in the future, he would never want to see this land again.

CHAPTER 8

STONE POISON

People who entered Coven Gate, have commenced the tasks that was given to them by Maureas' guards. "Prince Glarton," the Chief guard called him from behind, "Hope you had a good sleep." "Yes, I did," replied Glarton. Maurea had personally instructed the Chief to take care of Glarton and allot certain work to him. After glarton had his food, the chief instructed him to take care of the huts with broken roof. Chief was a little hesitant to say this, since he was asking a prince to work. Glarton did not react; he smiled and at once started the work. He went to the top of the huts, changed the broken thatched roof, arranged them properly and tied them with bast fibers.

Seeing the work of Glarton, the Chief was impressed and gradually opened an informal conversation with him. "What is the primary duty of a person who comes out of his hometown and enters a strange land?" Glarton glimpsed and wondered why the chief put forth such a question. After a pause he replied, "It depends on the person." The Chief guard was not satisfied with this answer.

The Chief pointed to a building far way and asked, "Glarton, do you see a tall building out there?"

"Yes, I do."

"That is Madiantes Institute, the place you want to go for learning."

At a distance Glarton could see the top part of a huge building. To increase the pressure, the Chief probed further, "Those who enter this border: may be rich or poor, prominent person or impostor; once he enters the Coven Gate, he is treated as a common man. They have to work on daily tasks." Glarton smiled and responded, "I do understand. Tell me, what I have to do next?"

The Chief was glad to hear this, "Clean all the dry leaves at the forepart and around the huts." Hearing this, Glarton was little hesitant and retreated. Remembering his fathers' words, 'When situations are not familiar and difficult, have patience and willingness to compromise and adapt,' he stepped forward and completed the cleaning work. In the middle of the day, the meal was provided. Glarton was again instructed to assist in setting up the table. Without any delay, Glarton performed all the duties.

In the evening, due to full day of work, Glarton was tired and was resting in his hut. As he went to lie down, he was disturbed by the sound of fight going on in the adjacent hut. He came out of his hut and saw a couple fighting in front of their hut. The man was shouting at his wife and threatening to hit her. Glarton enquired what was going on, and spoke to the man separately and solved the fight. He returned to his hut and slept.

Within few minutes he again heard some noise. He came out of the hut and saw at a distance; an outsider shouting at one of Maureas' workers. He was a young man who seemed scared and was trying to explain, whilst the foreigner did not let him speak and continued shouting. When Glarton reached, the outsider left the place. He queried the worker, "What happened here? Why was the man shouting?"

With hesitation he replied, "Nothing important, I was asking him questions and he got angry." Glarton said with gaze, "I can see you are scared. Do not be. Remember you are doing your work which was allotted by Mother Maurea. Therefore, tell me what has happened, and allow me to help you."

"He entered the Coven Gate today. He was not giving proper information regarding the purpose, hence the Chief commanded me to talk to him. All he disclosed was, he is a fugitive who wants to work and earn a living. He did not say much about his past. For me: his appearance, his accessories, his emotions and his actions, does not go with what he informed. He does not look like an honest man. I have to discuss this with the Chief but I wonder how the Chief would perceive it?"

Glarton said, "There is a method to know his innate behavior."

"How?"

"Ask one of your fellow workers, whom that man has not seen, to give a false appearance of being an innocent trader who is desperate and in need of money. He is willing to do anything to enhance his present situation. If the outsider recommends unlawful methods, then you can decide." The worker conveyed his gratitude to Glarton.

Early morning a guard approached Glarton in his hut and informed that someone has come to meet him and is waiting in Mothers' hut. Glarton followed the guard to the hut. He bowed and said, "Salutation Mother Maurea." Maurea bowed to him and then pointed her finger to the end of the hut, where Camigo was sitting. Glarton went closer to him, gazed at him for a while and then said, "Salutation uncle Camigo. Glad to meet you after a very long time."

Camigo hugged him, "Oh! Dear Prince, I am glad you do remember me. You look more like your father, my good old friend King Themton. How is he?"

"He is good."

Camigo turned to Mother and complemented, "I thank you for sending me a message and taking care of Prince Glarton." She bowed to accept his gratitude.

Camigo suggested, "Prince Glarton, with her permission, we can begin our journey at the earliest."

Glarton asked, "Mother Maurea, I thank you for having me here for the past three days. Can I enter Coven?"

Maurea smiled, patted him on his shoulder and said, "Being the son of a King alone does not define him as a Prince. He should possess the qualities of a future king. He must prove himself to be eligible to take upon the Kingdom. In the past two days, irrespective of being a Prince, you completed all the tasks allotted to you without any complain. When there was a fight going on in your neighboring hut, rather than giving importance to rest, you immediately came out and solved it. Over and above, I was informed that you even helped one of my workers in taking care of a situation. These prove that you do not think any work as inferior and you take people as the priority and shall take care. You can enter Coven."

She turned to Camigo and said, "Kindly stay for a meal and thence you both can continue your journey." Camigo and Glarton agreed. After a while, when Glarton was about to start, Mother Maurea came to his hut.

"Mother Maurea, I am much honored because of your arrival," said Glarton.

"There is something I want to give you, Prince." She handed him a small golden cloth pouch, which was tied by a thread. He opened it and saw a small stone. An oval crystal stone, smooth and shiny, with a sky-blue inner core. Glarton was surprised looking at it and after a short pause he asked, "When I was a child, my father told me a story about the Crystal Stone. A valuable stone in the South Island, which has been brought up from the deep ocean by a heavenly body. It was cut into two parts because of a greed. Is it true? Is this one half of the Crystal Stone?"

Maurea replied, "Yes, it is true and this is one of the halves. It was given to me by a person as a token of respect for my kindness." She turned to the window and gazing at the sunlight she continued, "Prince, this is a special stone, which can glow in the dark. The strength of this stone is; it can change into a blue stone when the person holding this either carries a poisonous substance or the person himself has been poisoned."

"I thank you for giving me this stone, Mother Maurea. Can I ask you something?"

"Yes."

"May I know what is the strength of another stone?"

With a worried face she disclosed, "A person possessing the stone, if desires to change to another person, all he has to do is hold the stone in his hand and look at that person, he can immediately change."

CHAPTER 9

MADIANTES

Glarton and Camigo started from Coven Gate riding on horse brought by Camigo. They were moving towards South-West to reach the border between Zeulean and Lumbian community. The route was fabulous with vast agricultural lands, trees with many beautiful flowers and colorful birds. Camigos' house was located at the foothills of Mount Agua. Despite being a small house, it had objects adorning the house. Handcrafted items were garnishing the entrance and walls of the house. His wife and their fifteen-year-old daughter were happy to receive him. They offered him a feast.

On the following morning, Glarton bowed to Camigo for his help and rode east towards the institute. Camigo did not accompany him because of the message he got from King Themton. On the way, Glarton was recollecting what Camigo told him about Sir Urases. Urases was born in a farmers' family who made an average living. Since childhood he had strong aptitude for gaining knowledge. In addition, he was excellent in different fighting skills. Seeing his hard work and intelligence, his master recommended further learning.

When Sir Urases was fourteen, he began inquiring about philosophy. Between the age of fifteen and twenty-one, he has been to Coven and Brozin to acquire excellent training from three great teachers of his time. At twenty-five, he established himself as a great Master of Coven. He got married and they had a beautiful daughter. He started his own academy - "Madiantes" meaning Master-Student; located at the North East part of Zeulean community, not farthest from the Coven Gate. For the past 20 years, he had trained many students from Coven, and its neighboring territories. He is an honest man with a strong heart, who supports his widowed sister, and her only son.

Glarton reached Madiantes before nightfall. It had a huge building in the center, which is accompanied by two small buildings on either side. In front of these buildings laid a vast land, which was used for training. Behind the central building is a house where the master and his family lived. The entire place was enclosed in a fence consisting of long rocks with sharp edges.

On the top corners of the building, there were tall thick sticks with its end bearing oil cloths, which was burning flame and illuminating the area. Inside, the entire place was glowing with candles on tables, torches on the walls, oil lanterns and lamps in the ceiling. The shimmering stars in the sky, and the gentle sway of the candle flames with the chill breeze, were setting a romantic air. Glarton dismounted from the horse and walked towards the central building.

When his eyes were glancing from the ground floor to the top, something on the first floor stopped him. A face, a beautiful face of a girl at the window. She was standing beside the window, seems to be sorting papyrus paper on the table. The young woman was standing with her face towards the window. She was staring at him with glittering eyes and shining cheeks. Glarton could not take his eyes off her face. For an instant, he forgot himself, the place, and everything. She turned back and continued her work. Glarton did not see her face clearly; therefore, he murmured,

A face,
An unseen face.
A face,
I shall die for.
A face,
I did not get enough off.
Turn, turn and look at me."

Immediately, she turned to the window, as if she can hear him. She glanced outside, but did not look at him; and left the room. Suddenly, a sharp arrow from the same window struck Glartons' heart. Gasping for air, he looked down at his chest. There was no arrow, no bleeding, no pain, rather a sense of pleasant disturbance. He realized, for the first time, he has fallen for a girl.

Glarton heard someone talking. It seems he was in a different world and someone dragged him to the real world. A man said, "Salutations Sir."

Glarton gave a difficult smile and replied, "Salutations Sir."

"May I know who you are?"

"I am Prince Glarton from Azunt, Kingdom of North Island. I have come here to meet Sir Urases."

The person requested Glarton to enter and be seated. After Glarton sat down, the person went to the rear of the room, opened a door and went inside. After few minutes, a tall and well-built man appeared, followed by the person. "Salutations Prince Glarton. I am Urases," said the tall man. Seeing the grand appearance of Urases, Glarton involuntarily stood up.

A calm face with a powerful aura around it. A flat forehead, with thick grey eyebrows, small eyes with sharp gaze, long nose, and small thin lips. The greyish white hair on his head, on his upper lip and around the chin showed the years of his experience. The master was wearing a long white robe. A red color cloth wrapped around his body from right shoulder diagonally covering the chest and going under left arm and came over his back, and ended around his right forearm.

"Salutations, Sir Urases. It is an honor to meet you."

"I Welcome you to Madiantes. Your father, Monarch Themton, sent me a message regarding your arrival. You can stay on the left side building." Glarton thanked him, who remained turning back as if he was expecting someone. A young woman came and Urases introduced, "This is my daughter Rhea. She helps me in my work."

Seeing her, Glarton heart was jumping up and down like a small boy shouting, 'The face, the same face!' Looking at Glarton, Urases said, "He is Prince Glarton from the North Island."

"Salu…salutations, Rhea." As he was enchanted, it was difficult for him to put words together.

Rhea smiled and said, "Salutations."

Sir Urases said, "Glarton, whenever I am unavailable, you can pass on any important message through my daughter. Now, have your supper and rest. We shall meet tomorrow morning."

The person at the entrance guided Glarton to the left side building. That night Glarton could not sleep. When he tried to close his eyes, Rheas' face disturbed his sleep: the blue eyes, fish shaped eyelids, well positioned nose, rose colored soft lips, and rounded chin. She would be six feet tall with lemon color complexion and properly curved body. She had a long and thick black color hair which was nicely adorned with beads at the top and bottom. Her neck was adorned by pearl chain with a matching pearl chain around her left wrist and short pearl chain on her right ankle. She was wearing a tight tunic with a rope around the hip and a skirt till her ankle. Glarton kept thinking about the events that happened from the moment he saw her at the window till her smile, and the word, 'Salutations.'

CHAPTER 10

LOVE OR ETHIC

"His name is Glarton. He is the son of King Themton, a disciplined king ruling Kingdom of Azunt." At home, Urases was talking to his sister about the new scholar.

Urases' sister said, "I have heard of King Themton; renowned for being a simple person. I have also heard that his Queen has passed away long time ago!"

"Yes, she passed away."

"How is the prince?"

"Like his father, Glarton seems to be a simple man; he does not carry any weight of being a Prince," added Urases. Rhea who was in the adjacent room was hearing them.

The home had two portions; the front was occupied by the master, and his daughter Rhea, and the rear portion was occupied by his elder sister and her son, Perses. Sister lost her husband when Perses was 5 years old and since then they have been staying with Urases. Perses has high regard for his uncle.

Rhea went to her chamber, laid on her bed and was recalling the events that happened in the evening. It seemed as not far from a dream; she could not believe it was real. In the first-floor room, when she was trying to clean the papyrus papers on the table, she became aware of a pair of eyes staring at her. Outside the building, towards her right, with the available dim light she could recognize someone was standing. As it was not very clear, she carried on with her work.

For unknown reason, her heart reminded her that she needs to look again. When she did, there were two attractive eyes, trying to pull her with its gaze. She could not understand the reason of why her heart was beating fast. 'Rhea,' she heard her fathers' voice so she left the room. In her fathers' working chamber her ears were hearing him, while her mind was trying to frame the face she saw outside the window. Her thought was going through the graciously flowing hair on the shoulder, the smile on the lips, and those attractive eyes.

She was asking herself, what am I doing? Why am I thinking like this? Who is he? Why was he looking at me intensely? I will be nineteen years old in a month, is this appropriate? While she was questioning herself, her father instructed her to follow him. After reaching the entrance, she was shocked to see the same face. Since her father was there, she did not have the strength to look at him longer. Lying on her bed, Rhea kept murmuring,

"Glarton.., Prince Glarton.., Glarton." Rhea was waiting for the sun to rise.

As Rhea was thinking about Glarton; in another room, Perses, her aunts' son was dreaming about Rhea. Perses was madly in love with Rhea. He had a portrait of her, which he had hidden behind his portrait, hanging on the wall. Every night, before going to sleep, he looks at her portrait. Since childhood, they were accustomed to play together as good friends. When they entered teenage, Perses' view on her changed. It was not his fault except his companions, whom often praised him of his looks, and beauty of Rhea and how they both shall make a great couple.

As Rhea lost her mother when she was 10 years old, it was her fathers' sister who took care of her. Now, he has turned twenty and she being eighteen, Perses desired to marry her. Even Perses mother was not aware of this. Many girls were attracted towards him for his tall slender but hard body, which was covered by tunic with surcoat and hose. Whenever he conversed with girls, rather than listening they admired his innocent face, the reddish black hair falling on his forehead, the wide attractive eyes, and the excessive movement of his hand and body while talking.

Perses excelled in attracting any girl which he desired and the girls in return believed that he is honest. He was marvelous with his favorite musical instrument, the recorder, which is a wind pipe instrument. During any gathering; Perses created his own poem, sang and played the recorder. There will be silence till he finishes his performance. One of his poems which was renowned by his friends was,

'Thousands of blooms, my friend,

Do not delay to taste.

Limit with just one, my friend,

You lose the taste in haste.'

Perses was proud and demanding. Girls, he has come across did not worry about it except one girl, Rhea, who not only disliked but also hated it the most. Often, she had mentioned to him politely and seldom she has mentioned to him angrily. Perses neither took them seriously nor was upset with Rhea for accusing him. As much as possible, he ensured his bad reputations did not reach her ears.

In the morning, Glarton went to the center building. Sir Urases have commenced his training for his scholars. In one corner of the ground, few were practicing bow and arrow, some with sword and shield, and the rest with spears. On the other corner, pupils were practicing marital arts, fighting methods without using any weapons. In front of the right side building a Master was teaching fundamental principles of fighting and its various methods.

Glarton bowed to Sir Urases, who nodded his head and gestured Glarton to follow him to the forepart of the left side building.

Sir Urases said, "Before going to your first day of teaching, I want to ask you a question."

Glarton responded, "Yes, Sir Urases."

"Being a Prince, you would have endured substantial training and teaching; may I ask, what do you hope to learn from here?"

"Yes, I have received extensive training from great Masters of my land. But I want to learn and hone my skills and wisdom from the greatest master of this world, so that I can fulfill my destiny. I have heard greatly about you and your academy that there is nothing else a person needs to learn once he is trained by Sir Urases."

Urases asked, "What is your destiny?"

"To unite all the kingdoms of the North Island and rule under one throne."

"For what?" asked Urases slyly.

Glarton answered, "Azunt is the smallest kingdom in the North Island. Our merchants have to go to neighboring territories to trade and make their earning. Unfortunately, there are lots of restrictions for that. Without a doubt, Azunt, and few neighboring territories dislike these restrictions. These decrees were imposed by King Ialkrit of Nosoe. The minor kingdoms are afraid to raise voice against Nosoe because it is a huge and powerful dynasty. Dissenters from surrounding territories were either punished cruelly or even killed. I aspire to change this condition where every kingdom in the North Island should be equal and safe."

"A noble cause which may be difficult but not impossible. Hmm…, Glarton tell me which weapons do you wield ably?" asked Urases.

"Sword, bow, glaive, and spears, on ground and on horseback. Whereas I have much to learn in fighting without weapons. Sir, can you teach me everything so that I can excel in all of it."

"For a pupil to learn from a master, it is necessary to surrender to the master. To learn from nothing, he has to empty his pride. I hope you have both the qualities. Here, take your sword and show me what you can do with it."

Urases gestured one of his pupils to combat with Glarton. From the scabbard, Glarton removed the sword which was given by his father. Glarton and the pupil started swinging their sword. The sharp clang sound of the swords was attracting others to look at them. Urases was seeing Glartons' grip at the hilt of the sword, the speed, wielding of the sword, and his leg movements concur with his hand. In less time, Glarton made the other to drop the sword.

Urases said, "Glarton. I will begin teaching you some crucial steps of sword attack and other martial fighting methods."

Days went by, Urases and his assistants taught the various intense methods. Within few days Glarton learned and mastered it. Urases admired his quick and enthusiastic nature.

One day on the practicing ground Urases asked, "Glarton, using bow have you ever hit a moving object?"

"Yes, I have."

"What if the moving object, goes up and down as well as from side to side?" Glarton denied of such a practice.

At one corner of the practicing ground there was a tall and thick stem that had a hand lever. A long stick was placed on this stem. This stick had four stones placed on top of it at equal distance. A small wooden plate was hanging from each stone on a rope. These ropes were connected to the lever through the stone. On rotation of the lever, the plates moved up and down due to the stones and as well as side to side.

Urases asked Glarton to aim with his bow, and as he was aiming at the plate, Urases ordered, "Shoot". Glarton released the arrow from his bow. It went fast and hit the plate. Glarton was happy, while Urases was not. He expected the arrow to pierce the center of the wood plate and not just touch it.

In the following days, Urases gave more training, which was intense. Glarton was longing to see his family and home town. But he stayed focused and learned earnestly. With the passing days, Glarton did it with ease and was starting to become more competent. Urases was happy with Glartons' performance.

Once in a while, Glarton and Rhea got opportunity to meet. If one of them got the courage to see, the other did not. They both wanted to convey their feelings for each other, but they were hesitant. On the completion of his first year, Urases wanted Glarton to come home for a supper. Glarton was highly pleased, since he was waiting for an opportunity to meet Rhea. Due to the intense learning in the past one year, he did not take additional effort to meet Rhea or stated his love for her.

In the evening, he adorned himself with expensive robe and left his building and walked towards Urases' home. As he was walking, all he could think was; will Rhea accept my love? Is this right? Is it ethical to fall in love with my masters' daughter? What if Urases finds out and ask me to depart Coven? Shall this cause shame for my kingdom? Lots of questions arose in his mind and he was worried.

He reached Urases' home and with hesitation called out, "Sir, Sir." On hearing Glartons' voice, Rhea who was in her room, came running to the entrance. On seeing her father approaching, she slowed down and stopped few feet away. Urases welcomed Glarton and asked him to sit. They were talking about the training and Coven. After a while, they sat for supper. Urases' sister and a male servant served the meal.

Rhea was standing near the kitchen, helping in passing the dishes from the kitchen. She was glancing at Glarton every now and then, without her father noticing it. He did not return her look, rather he looked at Urases. Rhea was eagerly waiting for her father to call out her name, so that she could come in front of Glarton. It happened. Rhea father called her to serve tea after supper. Unfortunately, Glarton did not look at Rhea even once and left without showing any gesture.

Rhea was disappointed. At night she could not sleep and kept crying. She tried to comfort herself; sadly, she could not. She assumed that Glarton does not want to reciprocate her feelings towards him. In the following days, whenever Glarton and Rhea came across, Rhea did not see him at all. Glarton understood that Rhea is upset with him and decided to put a stop for these misunderstandings. He decided to meet her and open up his heart, in spite of all obstacles.

CHAPTER 11

IT IS LOVE!

Pupils, after training, usually cross the center building to go to the left side dormitory. One evening, Glarton waited at the forepart of the center building hoping to see Rhea. He was lucky; she was in the same room on the first floor where he saw her for the first time. Glarton entered the building, and went to the first floor to her room. Glarton stood at the entrance of the room admiring her beauty.

The beautiful pearls hanging on her ears were shining and a small hair from her head ended beautifully curling over her cheek. The white shirt with frills around the neck, and wrist enhanced her beauty. The full-length blue skirt with white frills at the end gave nice curve to her body. All his heart wished was to stand there and keep looking at her forever.

Rhea was arranging the bows and putting arrows in quiver. She sensed someone standing near the door and staring at her. She turned and saw Glarton. Her heart started to beat fast. A mild tremble flowed from her head to toe. She spoke to him in a soft tone, "Salutations Prince Glarton." Glarton grinned and replied, "Salutations Rhea. May I come in?"

"Yes, come in."

He entered and sat on the chair opposite to her. She was standing and wondering with palpitation. The setting sun ray through the window fell on her face, making it glow. Glarton could not take his eyes off her face. Looking at her eyes, it was evident that she was holding his gaze. Eyes were locked and exchanging looks. After few minutes, Rhea broke the silence by clearing her throat, "Ahem."

Glarton gulped, "Rhea, there is something I want to tell you. It is …" He could not continue. Rhea understood his hesitation; she begged, "You can tell me anything…?" Glarton was little relaxed.

He stood up went to the window and looked at Rhea and said, "The first day when I entered this place, I saw a beautiful face standing at this same window. A face, I have never seen in my life; for a brief moment, the face was staring at me. I was pleasantly affected and frozen. I have never undergone such an emotion before. A new feeling, hmmm... marvelous."

Glarton came near to her, he wanted to hold her hand, but he did not. He looked at the floor, then at the window and then into her eyes and blurted out, "Rhea, I am not able to find the proper words to say what I am feeling. It is…, as if my soul has been searching for something and it found." After uttering these he heaved a sigh of relief, "Hoo."

Rhea was happy that finally Glarton is opening his heart to convey his feelings. She was shocked as well since, she could not believe this is happening. The reason was his action during the supper. She did not want to assume or ask so, she maintained silence.

After a pause, Glarton continued, "There are moments, when we truly get attracted to a person. Nobody knows why it happens. Do not think I am.. mm being un… unreasonable!" He was stammering, "Rhea, it could be your face, your eyes, or your smile. I can keep on saying." Glarton went little closer to Rhea, fixed his gaze on hers' and whispered, "Rhea I am in love with you."

Rhea was immensely joyful; smiling and her cheeks becoming red with shyness. Her heart began saying, 'Ho! I waited more than a year to hear this from you. What took you so long?' While lips were giving a narrow smile, their eyes continued talking. They advanced closer to each other. Rhea could sense his true love for her. His eyes were not lying. Glarton touched her cheeks with his fingers. Rhea was speechless; she smiled and closed her eyes.

Suddenly, he withdrew his hand, turned away and sighed, "You are my Masters' daughter, I do not know if it is right to love you. For this reason, when I came to your home, I was unable to look at you in the presence of the Master." In her heart, Rhea admired his honesty. She too had similar concern.

Glarton turned back to Rhea, and holding her hand he assured, "Rhea, at this moment my heart says not to let go of these hands forever, take you in my arms, care for you more than anything in this world and love you more than myself." He gave a pause and demanded, "I have shown you what I feel about you. Often, your eyes have spoken to me. But now open your mouth and tell me what is in your heart."

Rhea gazed at him, while her lips were struggling to open up. She stood still and did not utter anything. She was longing to say many things to him. Lot many thoughts flooded her at the same time and so her lips were sealed. Glarton could not understand the silence. He pleaded, "Rhea, say something, this silence is killing me."

Rhea was trying hard to pull the words out of her throat. Glarton continued, "Do you need some time to decide? Give me an answer tomorrow, at sunrise. I will be waiting at the same place where I saw you for the first time." He walked out of the room.

Rhea raised her hand to stop him and say how much she loved him. She almost went forward to stop him, but then she heard footsteps outside the door. One of the maids was nearing her room. She lowered her hand and sat on a chair. Glarton did not know that she tried to stop him.

At the dormitory, as Glarton laid down to sleep, every second passed like a decade. 'Why she did not say anything? I thought she will be happy to realize my love for her. Does she love me? May be, she has hesitation of falling for her fathers' pupil?' These questions were troubling Glarton.

On the contrary, Rhea was feeling bad for letting go of a golden opportunity. In her room, she was irritated by the interruption caused by the sudden entrance of the maid in to her room. Rhea wished to be loved, truly loved by a man who treats her as the one and everything for him. She also realized Glarton is the special someone for her.

Whenever Glarton looked at Rhea, she could see his eyes glowing with deep feelings for her. Sometimes, he looked at her as if he has known her for years. Her soul was waiting longer than a year to hear from Glarton and in the evening when he shared his affection, the brim of Rheas' heart was overflowing with joy, making her go blank.

The next morning, Rhea got ready early. She went to the center building. In her room, she stood in front of the same window and began rehearsing on what to say, and how to say. Every now and then she kept looking outside through the window. Soon, she saw him coming from the dormitory. Quickly, she left the room, ran down the stairs and stopped at the entrance of the building.

Glarton was glad to see Rhea, who was breathing heavily. She approached him, thinking about her words. She could not remember any of those words. She went close to him, leaned forward and rested her head on his shoulder. Slowly she lifted her head towards his eyes and whispered, "First time when I saw you from my room, I felt you are my special … I know nobody can love me or care for me more than you do. I love you."

Glarton could not believe his own ears. To ensure it is not a dream; he touched her right hand which was resting on his shoulder. She quickly dragged herself away, and smiled. Glarton put his hands around her hips and pulled her closer to his face. Both exchanged looks full of love. Glarton gently pressed her lips with his lips. Realizing what was going on, she blushed, stepped back, and ran in to the building. Glarton felt himself melting away.

Rhea went inside the building and to her room. She sat down, and gasped for air. Her heart was jumping up and down and her mind was restless. She was reminding herself not to get out of control. From a strictly close and conservative community, it was not allowed for a man and woman to meet alone before marriage. What if father finds out, ho!!I should be careful. She peeped outside the window. She was relieved that nobody was there.

Unfortunately, a pair of eyes stayed watching everything from a distance. The eyes belonged to Perses' best friend. He began running and stopped only in forepart of Perses' home. Perses was getting ready to go to the practicing ground. He was surprised to see his friend, so early in the morning.

CHAPTER 12

JEALOUSY

"Salutations my friend." The man did not wait for a second, he pulled Perses outside the home and pushed him to a side and told everything he saw in front of the center building. As his friend was reporting, inspite of Perses blood was boiling, he did not respond rather he patted him on his shoulder. Also, he thanked his friend for reporting the incident and requested him not to talk about this to anyone.

Once his friend left, Perses went inside the house, and sat on the floor. He sensed a deep and sharp cut on his stomach which climbed up to his heart and pierced it. In the next few minutes, he could not relax himself from this pain. He wanted to scream out his anger but he swallowed it with difficulty. After a while he stood up and went to the training area. He decided to approach Glarton and threaten him.

After finishing the training, as usual Glarton went to his room. He saw Perses standing outside his room. Glarton said, "Salutations Perses. How are you?" Perses was silent and remained glaring at Glarton. He signaled Glarton to go inside his room. After entering, Perses kept pacing inside the room. Glarton sensed something was wrong, and doubted whether it could be related to him and Rhea.

Glarton asked, "Perses, is there anything you want to talk?"

"Hmm.! Nothing Glarton. Hope you are feeling safe here!"

"What?"

Perses repeated, "Are you safe here?"

"I am safe here. Why?"

"You have come here from far away, leaving your palace, home land and your family."

"Yes, I have and your concern is…!"

In a firm manner Perses stated, "Sir Urases has informed me that you have come to Coven to get training. It is not uncommon to get carried away with unnecessary distractions, although you should not. Do not forget the purpose for which you are here." Perses came too close to Glarton and with his eyes fixed on Glartons' eyes, he said, "Prince Glarton, finish your training, and go back to your territory. Only do that. As long as you are clear about this, you will be safe here."

Glarton clearly understood that it is about Rhea. He responded, "I thank you, Perses for reminding my purpose in Madiantes. Is there anything more?"

"Nothing more, as long as you do not do anything more."

Perses marched out of the room with anger. Glarton can understand his anger, because in the conservative Coven community they do not encourage their women marrying men from other community.

Next day morning Glarton met Rhea at the same place and narrated the conversation he had with Perses. "What? How did he find out? I am certain he will create some trouble," said Rhea

"My dear, why are you worried about Perses. I know it is the community rule to.."

Rhea stopped Glarton by saying, "Perses wants to marry me."

"What?"

"Few times, he has indirectly talked about his love for me. Many times, I have directly told him not to have such kind of affection towards me. Actually, I dislike his attitude."

"Ho! So, this is the reason. Now I can understand why Perses was furious while talking to me."

"Perses will not accept our love, rather…" Rhea gave a pause and completed, "He will inform my father about us." Holding his hand, she said, "I am afraid of my father indeed."

"Rhea, I worry the same. Your father, my master shall not agree to this. But I will talk to him."

"What if he does not agree?"

Glarton adorned his hand with her beautiful face and said, "My dear, I will not give up trying." He then embraced her and was thinking 'How Perses came to know about us?'

Almost 2 years back, along with few scholars, Perses went for an annual tournament at Brozin Kingdom. This tournament occurs every year, and takes place at different parts of the South Island. While returning to Coven, they rested in a village. Perses heard few village girls talking in a nearby land. He was yearning to see the faces of those voice. As he could not control himself, he told others to carry on. Being known for his behavior, they left him and moved forward.

Perses left his horse under a huge tree, took his bag and climbed up for a better view. There were two ladies throwing and catching small tender coconuts among them. Perses sat on a comfortable portion on the tree and enjoyed seeing the girls jumping and running. Suddenly, he perceived something else on the tree, which was trying to approach him. He turned and stared towards the hissing sound. There was a yellow snake, which was approaching him.

Perses began to climb down the tree. He saw the snake following him down the branch. He began to come down fast, so did the snake. He was scared because he had no weapon to defend himself. He quickly got down the tree and jumped on the ground. When he jumped, he heard the snake hiss loudly, as if it was in pain or trying to scare Perses. He ran towards the place where he left his horse, to snatch his sword and shield. He could not find the horse in the spot where he left it.

Perses started running through the grass and he took a wooden log from the ground and threw it on the snake. For a second it stopped in pain and then it became furious and chased him faster. He continued picking up the stones, woods and things which he found on the path and threw it on the snake. Sadly, nothing could stop it. At one-point Perses slipped on a mud and fell on the ground and injured his left knee. "Aah!" He screamed of pain. Now he knew nothing can stop the snake. The snake came near him and opened its mouth wide.

"Hooooshh!!" A sound and next moment the snake was on the ground. An arrow struck its open mouth, followed by few more arrows piercing the snake head and killed it. Perses looked at the direction of the source and saw a man, who was approaching him. The man extended his left hand and lifted Perses.

Perses stood up and said, "I thank you for saving my life. My name is Perses and you are?"

The man replied, "Sir, my n-n-name is Ereblan. I see that your kn-n-nee is wounded, let me help." Perses felt deep pity for Ereblan. With the available herbs present around, Ereblan prepared a medicament, applied on the knee and tied a long leaf around.

Ereblan was almost 6 feet tall, slightly built body, brown color skin, having a loose tunic with sleeves and tight bottom. He must be more or less 25 years old. He had a long cloth around his neck and a beautifully printed cloth wrapped around his right hand. Ereblan helped Perses to find his horse.

"Ereblan, you are of great help to me. I will never forget this. Are you from this place?" asked Perses.

"No, I am from a s-s-small village of Goptm, which is located in the N-n-north Island."

"What are you doing in Brozin?"

"I am a merchant. I lost my parents when I was a s-s-small boy. My aunt took care of me. Lately, s-s-she passed away. I came to Brozin in search of an earning."

"Ereblan, if there is any way I can help you, tell me."

"If you can help me to find a beginning, it would be helpful," replied Ereblan.

"Do not worry. Come with me to Coven. My uncle has a training academy. I shall request him to help you."

"I thank you, s-s-sir."

"You can call me Perses."

Ereblan said, "Perses."

Since then, Perses and Ereblan became good friends. Frequently, Ereblan has showed loyalty to Perses and Urases. He has efficiently completed the works assigned to him. At the Madiantes, many including Urases were impressed with Ereblans' sincerity and hard work. On the other day, the eyes that were watching Glarton and Rhea belonged to Ereblan, who informed Perses regarding their love.

CHAPTER 13

ANGER

As days passed by Glarton was highly attentive with his training and proved his capability in archery, sword, spear wielding and many such weapons. Seeing this, Urases decided to teach a unique fighting skill. "Glarton, I am going to teach you a special ancient fighting skill, Martial Dance, which only the Covenans know and may be a few outside this native have learnt." As Urases commenced the first class, Glarton saw it was different than what he was expecting. It was like a dance. It had a rhythmic movement of the body with kicks and jumps in between. He could not follow.

Urases understood this, "At the beginning, you shall find it different, because it resembles dance. This is good for stability; with more effort and frequent practice you can become more competent." Glarton tried to do it by reminding himself; step-1 move to the right, step-2 left, step-3 jump over the left side, step-4 bend down, and so on.

In the following weeks Urases ordered Glarton to practice day and night. Since he has completely surrendered to the master, he did not complain and continued practicing. Often, he reminded himself of his fathers' advice which was, 'The more you have patience and attention, the faster you can learn.'

Glarton developed a good balance of his body on one leg, and was able to do the steps in a smooth and continuous way. Urases taught him additional steps and group actions with others. Glarton started liking this type of martial art. In the following days he was gradually mastering it. Urases was feeling proud of Glarton, while at the same time, he perceived that Perses was behaving different.

Perses was learning Martial Dance for a while however, he was not showing interest in mastering it. Rather he kept finding fault with Glarton and told them in front of others. Urases understood that Perses may be getting jealous of Glarton. During the group practices, he showed anger to others by hurting them. Urases foresaw that Perses may misuse this learning hence, he ordered Perses to stop the training for a short time.

The annual tournament was planned to happen in a week. That year it was happening at Zeulean community at the ground of Madiantes. The community elders gathered to discuss the various activities about to happen on the day of the tournament. Every year, money was collected from different counties of Coven and a magnificent celebration was arranged. The tournament consisted of various forms of combat.

The students of Madiantes were excited to join the tournament. In front of all the students and workers, Urases proclaimed the name of the scholars who were chosen for different categories. Usually, one pupil is chosen for one category. However, this year, for the first time Glarton was chosen in two categories. This created problem among those who have been learning from Urases for years, even before Glarton has joined. The person for whom this was highly unacceptable was Perses. He discussed with Ereblan, who seemed to agree that Glarton should not be allowed to participate in two categories. On the same day, after supper, Perses went to meet Urases.

"Sir, I want to talk to you."

Urases replied, "Ho Perses! how often have I told you no to call me Sir when we are inside the house. Call me uncle."

"Uncle!"

"Yes, tell me what is troubling you?"

"Hm! nothing…. nothing is troubling me?"

"My boy, my boy," Urases smiled and continued, "I am familiar with you since you were a small boy. In the past few days, you are annoyed with something. Am I wrong?"

"Yes Uncle, it is been troubling me for many days and today it went over the brink."

Urases understood what he was addressing to, still he pretended not knowing. Perses controlled his anger and with a firm voice he said, "Uncle, today you proclaimed the names of the chosen pupils and…," he could not complete the sentence.

Urases asked, "And?"

"You mentioned Glartons' name in more than one category."

"Yes. I did."

"Concerning that, there is discontent among the students."

"Discontent! What for?"

"Many feel, it cannot be justified to select Glarton in both the categories, since it has never happened before."

In a calm voice Urases responded, "Yes, they are right. It is because I have never thought a person can do well in more than one."

"Uncle, I understand. There are many who have been learning from you for years. They are more capable than Glarton. They opine that you could have given them the same opportunity."

Urases smiled, and signed Perses to sit beside him. He looked straight into Perses eyes and asked, "Says who? You or them?" Perses got startled with this question, "No uncle, it is not me."

Urases asked, "Hmm… What do you think?"

"I think what they are feeling is correct. Can you think about it again?" He could not look at Urases face. Urases smiled and understood that Perses has made his friends feel the same. He stood up went to the window, looked outside at the silent night and stated, "As a teacher my decisions are always based purely on the trainees' ability and hard work. Glarton is chosen for two places and there is nothing to discuss."

Perses comprehended the soreness arising between him and his uncle. He still asked, "But uncle, can you try to," before he could complete his sentence, Urases said in a loud voice, "There is nothing to discuss further." Perses did not want to say anything out of rage, so he quickly left the house.

Next day while talking to his friends, Perses informed the conversation he had with the Master. Ereblan stated, "My friend, this is not righteous. Glarton s-s-should n-n-not be allowed to participate in two categories." Others also agreed to this.

Perses said, "What to do? The master says he is capable and hardworking."

Ereblan argued, "There are s-s-students who have all these. Honestly, I feel that you are more able than Glarton." Ereblan was gradually fueling the burning pride of Perses.

He signaled him to come close, then Ereblan whispered, "If he s-s-starts to s-s-show his s-s-strength at the tournament, Rhea may think highly about him. N-n-not only her, but this may also s-s-strongly affect the community elders who will be coming for the tournament. When they ascertain their love to the elders, they may n-n-not object. S-s-so, think, Perses." Ereblans' words kept repeating in Perses ears. The entire day Perses was angry and restless. In the evening, he again went to meet Urases and was determined to slander Glarton.

Lots of work needed to be done for the tournament so, in the evening Urases wanted Rhea to stay back in the center building for little longer. To inform this, Urases went to the center building and to the first floor to Rheas' room. When he entered, he saw Rhea standing beside the window and looking outside. He waited there for a while hoping Rhea to turn. She did not. She was looking happy, and smiling with shyness. He has never seen her happier like this. Wondering what could it be! Urases went near the window from behind her but not close to her. He stopped in shock to see the person she was looking at was Prince Glarton, who was also looking happier. Without saying anything he went to his room.

Already, Urases was upset with the problems of his students, adding to this, Rhea and Glarton. 'What is going on? Is my daughter in love with the Prince from the North Island? Perses likes my daughter, could this be the reason he was showing jealousy on Glarton? What will happen if others find out? What will be the response of King Themton?'

He sat down on his chair, leaned forward and supported his head with his hand on the table. After thinking about these for a while he decided, 'I am worried, whereas Rhea is happy. I have never seen her face happier like this. If they are truly in love with each other and shall be happy to lead a future together then, as a father, I have to support them.'

When Urases reached his house, he was shocked to see Perses waiting for him. He got worried. 'Why is he here? Is it to talk about Glarton and the tournament? Or could it be possible he wants to discuss about Rhea and Glarton!'

"Perses, I did not see you in the practicing ground today!"

Perses stood up, came near to Urases and said, "Uncle."

"Yes."

"Uncle."

"What is it, Perses?"

"There is something bad, I have to inform you. Hmm… the truth is I am little scared to tell you."

Urases now realized what it could be, so he undesired to talk about it. "Perses how is the training for the tournament going on?"

Perses replied, "It is going on as expected. I want to inform you," Urases stopped him and enquired concerning the training. Losing patience, Perses specified, "The matter is…..aghmmm… Rhea is a lovely girl, but innocent. She easily trusts others…,"

Again, Urases did not let him finish, "Yes, she is and also intelligent. Hence, whatever decision she makes, I shall be glad to support her." Making this firm statement, he gazed at Perses. He stood shocked; he realized that his uncle is aware of the love between Glarton and Rhea. No point in talking indirectly.

"Are you aware of the truth about Glarton?"

"Yes."

"What? You know and you are taking no action!"

"What action should I take, when I have accepted them."

Perses raged, "Uncle this is not agreeable. Our community may not allow it and, and…," he stammered and continued, "You understand my feelings towards Rhea. You …., you, should take care of this."

Urases got enraged and with a thunderous voice he declared, "Perses, Rhea is my daughter; I know how to take care of this. You may go now." Perses was speechless, frightened and left the place quietly.

CHAPTER 14

THE TOURNAMENT

On the day of the tournament various activities were going on at different corners of the field. It was a three-day tournament. The Covenans had a custom: in the evening before beginning the tournament, a tall, and thick wooden stick was planted on the four borders of the town of Coven. Each stick had a red flag at its end. This is an indication of a tournament beginning in the following days and no one at Coven can depart the territory. Those who goes against this restriction, is not allowed to enter again. The reason is, by crossing the border they are showing disrespect for the spirit of the tournament and the community elders.

On the first day, they had a grand welcome function for the community elders of Coven and the prominent people of their neighboring territories. Urases welcomed the guests by giving a long velvet cloth to each of them, as a sign of showing respect for them. Then he took the guests to the field and showed them the various fighting methods and weapons. The guests were happy and admired Urases for the effort.

In the evening, they had various amusements such as traditional dancing, singing, and drama. Scholars from various schools of different territories also participated. The local men and women dressed themselves lavishly to show the pride of Coven. When Rhea entered the place, most of the eyes in the crowd was on her. The pearls and flowers adorning her hair, the beads and stones embellishing her dress, made her look elegant and bright. Many were admiring the beauty of Rhea.

The pupils of Madiantes performed various cultural events, which were applauded by the guests and viewers. Urases was proud. Glarton was on and off the dais taking care of many works. Whenever he got an opportunity, his eyes were searching for Rhea and he could not stop himself from looking at her.

On the second day morning the martial combat began. There were both group tournament and individual competition. There were different levels and each filtered to choose the best fighters. By noon, three sets of students were chosen for group combat. One set had Glarton and two students from Madiantes. The second had three from neighboring territory and the third had Perses and two students from Madiantes. In group competition Glartons' team won whereas in the individual, to everyone's surprise, the final round had Glarton against Perses.

Since Urases knew the friction going on between Glarton and Perses about Rhea, he was not happy. He recommended to the judges and the elders to either declare both as the victors or withdraw both of them. The judges said if both fighters agree then they can accept. Glarton agreed with Urases, while Perses was not interested to withdraw. Moreover, he wanted to use this opportunity to show Rhea that he is stronger than Glarton.

Urases could not compel Perses to agree. He explained to the judges that the two fighters from the same academy pitted against each other could later cause some trouble. He requested them to cancel this round. The judges disagreed since Perse is not accepting to withdraw and wanted to fight. The judges also stated that either Perses or Glarton wins, the prize and pride will be for Coven. So, there is no reason for Urases to worry. Rhea was not happy about this as she knew that Perses will wantonly harm Glarton.

With the spread of the news regarding the last tournament happening between the two strong men of Madiantes; the entire Covenans gathered. The sun was getting ready to set down as if it was not interested to see this combat. Perses knew that Glarton was strongly competent with weapons whereas not skillful in physical combat.

He remembered Ereblans' words, 'Perses even if you win, Glarton might find different methods to impress Rhea. Glartons' prosperity and power s-s-s-hall make our Master to agree. My friend hurt him, hurt him in s-s-such a manner that he becomes a living corpse, thenceforth your uncle will disagree their marriage and will ask him to return."

As the fight commenced, Perses started attacking Glarton continously, like a mad man. Several did not agree to this and shouted to stop. Whereas, those who were Covenans and friends of Perses, was encouraging him to continue. Rhea and Urases, who were viewing the fight from a higher platform, were worried. Rheas' eyes were filled with tears, which she did not let down. Glarton knew that Perses was skillful in martial combat hence, the only choice to defend him is to drain Perses' energy.

Perses was hurting Glarton in a manner to avoid any breach of rules. After some duration, Perses became tired, on the contrary Glarton kept going. Perses unfortunately did not gauge Glartons' ability to withstand. Due to the violent hit, kick, pulling and throwing on the floor, Glarton was bleeding on the face, knees, and shoulders. His body was aching with pain. Glarton was getting trained in fights for a year, whereas Perses was learning this for many years.

Urases knew that Perses is skillful in physical combat. However, he also knew that Glarton has a better withstanding capability, which he has never seen in any of his pupils. It was for this reason Urases chose Glarton in two categories of the tournament.

The crowd was surprised to see how Glarton was rising up even after receiving heavy beatings. Now Perses was getting irritated. He paused for a moment wondering how

Glarton was able to rise up. Glarton smiled, with blood oozing from his nose and mouth. After understanding the different attacks of the adversary, Glarton was getting certain about his victory. He ran towards Perses, who got ready and gave a strong kick. Glarton defended Perses blow and gave him back with his hand and leg at the same time. Perses flew in the air and fell on the mud.

An unbearable sharp pain passed from his spinal cord to his legs. Now he realized that Glarton was getting all the beatings only to find out his movements. He arose with difficulty, stood, and again got a blow from Glarton. Perses rolled on the ground. Since he already lost his strength by giving unceasing attacks to Glarton, he doubted about his win.

Lying on the ground Perses looked at Rhea, who frowned in anger. He thought, 'A shameful situation.... No.... no! Not this look. If I am defeated..., aaagh...,'he felt a rage inside him. Then he looked at the spectators. 'Glarton does not belong to this Island hence, if he gets defeated it will not affect him much. If I am defeated; my own people shall despise me. It will cause my everyday life painful. I should have tried to win Rheas' love by some other manner.' He tried to stand up.

Nothing is left, he was mentally ready to get the last punch and lay still on the ground. Whereas, Glarton stood still. Perses could see that Glarton was in some thoughts. He was afraid that may be Glarton has decided to kill him. He tried to kick Glarton with his right leg; expecting a defending blow. Surprisingly, without defending, Glarton received the blow and fell on the ground. He rose; lifted his leg to attack. Instead of kicking fast he moved slowly. This gave Perses an opportunity to give a heavy kick on his chest, which made Glarton fell on the ground. This time he did not rise; laid on the ground and showed sign of being in agony. Up in the high platform, tears no more listening to Rhea, rolled down on her cheeks. Moments passed by, Glarton did not arise. The Judges declared Perses as the victor.

CHAPTER 15

HAPPY AND WORRIED

Everyone in the crowd were shouting and Perses friends lifted him for admiration. The elders approached and blessed him for the success. There was no pride on the face of Perses and Urases. For spectators, Glarton was growing weaker then he started to attack Perses. But in the end he became exhausted and finally Perses defeated Glarton. Both uncle and nephew certainly knew that the prince still had the ability to rise and fight. Rather, he chose to accept the blow and make Perses the victor.

That night Perses went to Glartons' room. He was hesitant to knock the door. He stood outside for a while; stepped back to return but then knocked the door. Glarton opened the door and welcomed him to come inside. There were many wounds on his body. Glarton sat in a corner; waiting for Perses to talk. Perses was quiet. Seeing this Glarton said, "Yes, Perses!"

Looking down Perses murmured, "Glarton the people and the judge thought I defeated you and declared me as the winner. Deep inside we both knew that you are the winner. If you would have given me one more blow, I would have fainted immediately. Rather, you gave up your rights."

Glarton gave a weak smile. Perses came near Glarton, sat down next to him and looking straight in to the eyes asked, "Why?"

"Perses, for Coven, I am an outsider; nobody knows me whereas you are from here. This is your land." He leaned back on the chair, "I will return after I am done with the training, whereas you have to live here and face your friends and Covenans every day." Perses was listening attentively.

Glarton continued, "I saw the way you looked at the crowd." He paused, leaned forward; looking at Perses, he said, "If you were defeated, it will affect you badly, which I think you cannot handle." These words chocked Perses intensely. He could not say anything, and left the room quietly with a burning rage. As he kept walking towards his home, he realized why Rhea chose Glarton and not him.

At home, Rhea was worried about Glarton. 'How is he feeling now? He was wounded and bleeding. Hope he had some medicine. Why did he allow Perses to defeat him? How could this happen?' She could not wait until morning. She wanted to know his present situation, immediately. As time passed by, she was becoming more restless. At the supper table, Urases saw that she did not eat properly. He knew that she is feeling restless regarding the prince. When she asked him, he replied that Glarton was taking rest and did not say anything more. She was not satisfied. She wanted to know more.

Rhea waited for her father to sleep. Then she took the lantern flame, quietly came out of her room, crossed the passage and went to the backyard. She wanted to go outside the home through the backdoor of the kitchen. She slowly and carefully opened the door, so it does not make any squeaky noise. As she put her right foot outside the door; "Is this the right time to meet Glarton?"

On hearing her fathers' voice from behind, she was frozen. Urases came close to her and said, "Rhea, come inside the house." She quietly entered the house; still, she did not look at him. Her head was down with shame.

"My dear daughter, I am aware of your strong affection towards Glarton. But I never expected such a deed from you. Rhea, the masters' daughter, sneaking out of her home in the middle of the night to meet one of the students! Is this a righteous action?"

Rhea was shocked on realizing that her father was aware of her love for Glarton. Still looking down she whispered, "Father, I apologize," saying this she knelt on the floor and began sobbing. Her tear droplets fell on the ground, beside her fathers' feet. "Father, I should not have tried to go out like this. But I could not help myself. Can you forgive me?"

Urases brushed Rheas' head and said, "Arise Rhea." He sat on the chair and asked her to sit beside him. "Look at me." She slowly lifted her head and looked at him, who fixed his eyes on her and questioned, "Do you honestly love him?" She was startled, since she never expected such a question from her father. She was scared to reply.

Urases asked again, "Do you?"

"Yes father, I do."

"From your action I can well see that. Is Glarton also earnest about you?"

Without a doubt she replied, "Yes father, he is."

"But, being a prince; the future king, will he honestly take you as his future Queen?"

"Yes, he will."

"My child, if you both see a future together and never give up on each other," with a smile on his face he continued, "Then I have no objection."

"Ho father!" Rhea hugged her father and said, "I thank you. I was worried a lot about your response. I am glad."

"Hmm…, What will happen when our elders come to know about this?" Rhea looked at her father, whose face became sad. Urases continued, "I am worried about that. There will be questions asked immediately after they find out."

Rhea asked, "Father, will this cause despair to you? I will apologize to the elders?"

"No, my dear. I will talk to them and find a good solution for your sake." Rhea was overwhelmed with happiness. She hugged him again and said, "I thank you father. Since I was a small girl, you have done many things for me. I wish to get more opportunities to serve you."

CHAPTER 16

AGREED AND ACCEPTED

On the third day of the tournament, there were demonstrations on how to use various weapons. This was done by the students from various Universities. Each university took two types of weapons. They were showing defensive and offensive stances. Glarton and Perses did not participate. Urases understood their situation and did not ask them the reason. Glarton and Perses were sitting with the crowd as spectators.

Rhea and Urases were looking at the performance from a higher platform. Since morning Rhea was eagerly waiting for an opportunity to meet Glarton. She wanted to meet him alone; to know his health and also to convey her fathers' approval. Unfortunately, she could not do it. One or two times when Glarton looked at her, she did signal him to meet her. But he could not understand that. As time passed by, she could no longer wait.

Rhea approached Glarton, who was talking to some men. She glimpsed at them and turned to Glarton, "Prince Glarton, Sir Urases was looking for you." Glarton was taken aback because just few moments earlier he had spoken to the master. Moreover, Rhea was addressing him as Prince Glarton. He understood that she wanted to talk to him privately. He playfully delayed it to see how she will respond, so he pretended a little.

"Truly?" questioned Glarton.

"Yes," replied Rhea.

"I shall meet him on the platform." Saying this he turned to take his step. She got irritated; raised her voice when she said, "No." Men who were around suspected something is going on between them so, they laughed. Rhea stared at them with anger; turned to Glarton, and with a stern voice demanded, "Can you meet him at the center building, now?"

Glarton smiled and agreed, "Yes, I shall."

He immediately went to the building. Few moments after Glarton left, Rhea sneaked out of the crowd and went towards the building. As she entered her room, Glarton who was standing behind the door, came near to her; put his arms around her hips and took her towards him and asked, "So, Sir Urases, what can I do for you?"

"Ho! You knew it! Why did you pretend?" saying this she tried to move away from him. Glarton laughed; pulled her again and tried to hug her. She looked at the wound on his face and hands and in a low voice asked, "Glarton, since yesterday evening I was worried about you. I wanted to know about your health." She leaned closer to his face and moved his hair to see the wound on his forehead.

"I had some pain," saying this he suddenly kissed her cheeks and continued, "Now I am feeling better."

Rhea looked down shyly and smiled. She gripped Glartons' right hand and pulled him to a corner. Glarton could not understand this quick action. Suddenly she hugged him. He hugged her back and whispered in her ears, "My sweetheart, if you are going to hug me like this, then I am happy to get wounded again and again."

She pushed him away gently, and narrated the conversation she had with her father. Glarton was glad to hear that their love got accepted by Sir Urases. He went near to Rhea and brushed her lips with his. She pushed him away and smiled.

"Rhea, I am glad that your father accepted our love for each other." He paused and continued, "I think, now it would be appropriate for me to talk to your father about our marriage." She nodded her head.

"I think now you should allow me to honor your lips again," saying this he tried to kiss her lips. His lips touched hers gently. She shivered and pushed him back. He looked down with disappointment. She went near to him, lifted his face; gave a closed mouth quick kiss on his lips. A sweet emotion passed through his body. He tried to hold her, but saying "No, no!" she left the room and ran back to the ground.

Glarton heart was jumping with happiness. In the night he kept rehearsing on: what to say to his master, how to say and what to answer. By staying in Coven for a long time, he understood their customs. He knew that the locals had a particular manner of getting married.

Next day evening, Glarton met Urases at the forepart of the center building. "Salutations Sir."

"Salutations Glarton."

"Sir, there is something personal I want to talk to you. Shall we talk now?

Urases could guess what it could be. He did not want others to hear their conversation. Hence, he recommended, "Yes, we can talk now. Hmm…, Shall we go to my study!" Glarton nodded his head. After entering the room, Urases sat in a chair.

Glarton spoke, "Sir, I should have told this before. My apology for delaying. I was hesitant and scared." Urases signaled Glarton to sit. But Glarton could not. He said, "Sir me and your daughter Rhea are in love with each other." Glarton gasped for air as he disliked to stammer with fear. He looked straight into his Masters' eyes and stated, "I truly want to marry your daughter and I know according to the custom here," he stopped, stood up, bowed his head and gulped, "Sir, I am here to ask your daughters' hand in marriage."

As a father, Urases was highly relieved. According to their custom, the family of the man should approach the family of the woman and ask her for marriage. If it happens the other way, it was seen as a shame for the girls' family. He was glad that Glarton took the first step. He knew he can trust Glarton.

Glarton said, "I am aware that you are my teacher; I am your student, so I am uncertain if this is proper. Sir, kindly hear me out. When I first met Rhea, I was not aware she is your daughter. I fell in love with her, not knowing her name or her relation with this academy." He finished by saying, "Actually, I met her before I met you."

Urases understood that Glarton is anxious. To calm him, he said, "Glarton, you do not fear. I absolutely understand. I know that my daughter Rhea loves you too. But…," with a worried voice he continued, "Glarton, you are a Prince. This relationship shall not be accepted by your father, King Themton or your people?"

"The truth is, I cannot promise that my fathers' response will be good. I am certain that he has always been supportive of my feelings. When my parents got married, my mother was from another kingdom. I can promise; if he does not agree, I will keep requesting him until he gives acceptance."

"I am glad to hear this." While Urases was happy to hear this but it was not giving a strong assurance. Therefore, he said, "According to our custom, I recommend that your father come here and talk to me about the marriage."

Glarton had doubts regarding this. In Azunt the custom is other way. The girls' father should approach. Also, being a king of Azunt, will he agree to come? He sat down on a chair. He was silent for some time. Then he looked at Urases and said, "I understand Sir. For this I have to go home and talk to my father. When can I go?"

"You are almost done with the training. Sooner, you can return to your territory."

CHAPTER 17

THE INK

Urases handed Glarton a quiver. It was looking different from the other regularly used quivers. It had a division inside. One side had medium sized arrows and other side had ink. The quiver seemed to be heavy, but on lifting it was light.

"Glarton this is an ordinary arrow but the ink is not. The arrow has to be lightly dipped in this ink and need to be shot with light force. The greatness is, the inked arrow once leaves the bow, it will not be seen for next several moments. As it goes in the wind, the air removes the ink from the arrow making it appear again."

"Sir, are you saying that the arrow would be invisible until it reaches the target?"

"Yes."

"Hmm…It will be like a sudden attack for the enemy!"

"Yes."

With impatient desire Glarton asked, "Sir, may I know what is this ink made up of?"

"Ha… Ha… Ha…" Urases laughed and said, "A secret. It is a secret. Only few elders of Coven still know the ingredients and they pass the secret to their heirs." Moving his head close to Glarton he whispered, "Rhea is one among them."

Glarton gave a closed-mouth smile and questioned, "Can I use an ordinary bow for this arrow? Or, Is there any special bow?"

"A special bow has to be used and you need to make it for yourself. Remember, since the arrow is being dipped in an ink, you need to make a bow in such a way that the bow does not absorb the ink when the arrow crosses it."

Glarton realized that the challenge is not making a bow, but in making the bow with something that does not absorb the ink from the arrow. He went around to different towns of Coven, enquired people and in the following days prepared a bow accordingly. He used the wood of a medicinal tree to make the bow. He anointed the center of the bow with the oil extracted from the brown seaweed of the river water. This avoids the bow absorbing the ink from the arrow. Holding the bow, Glarton proudly went to Urases and showed him. Urases taught him on how to use the dye and shoot the arrow.

"Glarton, you have learnt what I wanted you to learn. Hence, today I declare as the last day of your training," said Urases proudly. He gave Glarton a small pouch.

Glarton opened it and saw a small stone pot filled with ink.

"Is this for me?"

"Yes."

"But I thought...!"

"It is a gift for your hard work."

"I thank you, sir!"

"Remember, this ink is precious. It is not to be used for fun or for pride. So, Glarton promise me that you will use this ink only when there is a real threat for your life."

"I obey your words," saying this Glarton bowed to Urases.

People in the university came to know that Glarton has completed his training and will be returning to Azunt in the next few days. Perses approached Glarton and confessed, "Glarton, I was in love with Rhea. It is sad she never loved me. After realizing her love for you, I was jealous, jealous and jealous. Thenceforth, I found ways to hurt you and put you down. But you have always been a good person to me. I realized that your love is true." Haa... he exhaled heavily and told, "Glarton, you shall be leaving in two days, so, I requested Sir Urases to allow me to do a farewell tomorrow. He has approved so, you are coming."

"Perses, it takes great courage to confess something. Thanks for the gathering. I will be there."

"Good. For tomorrow I am going to cook one of the traditional sweets of Coven, specially for you."

"Ho! I thank you."

Before sunset, Glarton took Rhea to a waterfall which is at the eastern part of the Zeulean community. A tall gentle waterfall surrounded by mist, created by the splashing water, glimmered with the attracting rays of sun setting behind it. They both sat at the edge of the water stream; holding each other hand. Rhea dipped her feet into the cool water with her head resting on Glartons' shoulder.

Glarton saw the sun giving off its orange light, which was spreading in the sky. Rhea was enjoying the same reflection in the water. After looking at the beauty of the nature, he looked at Rhea and whispered, "Beautiful waterfall, beautiful sunset, beautiful Coven," before he could complete, Rhea looked above to meet his eyes, with one eye opened and other closed.

He understood, "My Rhea, my Rhea, your beauty is enthralling. You are the most beautiful of all these. This waterfall and sunset can only quench my thirst for a moment, but your beauty... forever." He kissed her on her forehead. She smiled and felt the warmth of his embrace engulfing her.

After a while of silence Glarton called, "Rhea…"

"Yes."

"How am I going to depart? I shall take many days to return. How can I be away from you?" These words made Rhea sad. He was feeling bad to see her being sad. "What happened dear?"

Rhea looked at him, filling her eyes with his face and said, "You will always be in my thoughts, Glarton."

"My love, each of my moment will pass only with your thoughts. Do not worry, I shall return with my father and ask your hand in marriage. Thenceforth…", he touched her cheeks gently with his lips and assured, "I will take you to Azunt as my Queen."

Rhea was happy to hear this. She whispered, "Until that happens my life is empty without you. I shall talk about my loneliness to the moon." They both looked at the sky. The blue color remined Glarton of the special stone which Maurea gave to him. As it looks beautiful and attractive, he assumed that she might be happy to keep it.

Glarton told, "Do not worry Rhea. You do not have to talk to the distant moon; you can talk to a small gift, which I will be giving you tonight after the gathering." She wanted to know more about it, but it was nightfall and she had to go home and get ready for the gathering. She responded, "Eagerly waiting. See you at the farewell."

CHAPTER 18

THE FAREWELL

The center building was emblazed with lights and festooned with flowers. People have gathered at the forepart of the building. At the center of the ground, deliciously prepared traditional foods were kept on a table. Musicians were performing music: some were dancing while some were having food and wine. Urases was sitting on a tall chair at a little raised platform. Glarton was sitting a little front of and on the side of Urases and Rhea was standing on the other side of Urases.

Rhea was looking extraordinarily beautiful. Her neck had a white pearl necklace with a red heart shaped pendant, round short ear rings, and the hair was collected and made as a nice bun. She wore a full length dark green dress which had prints at her chest, waist and knee levels. It was neither tight nor loose, yet it was perfect. The lights from the lantern and candle reflected on her face, enchancing her beauty. Glarton kept looking at her every now and then, without Urases becoming aware of it. Similarly, Rhea was also looking.

Urases signaled Rhea to come and sit next to him. She did and due to which Glarton could not glance at her. So, he made a gesture of disappointment and faced the other side. Rhea understood his action and giggled.

Perses, who came out of the side building, stood frozen looking at Rheas' beauty. He approached her and told, "You look wonderful. I have never seen you glowing like this."

"Perses, I thank you."

Perses went and sat beside Glarton. "Salutations Glarton. Hope you like the gathering!"

"Salutations Perses. It is wonderful, but one thing is missing."

"What?"

"The special sweet you mentioned to offer me." Both Glarton and Perses laughed loud. Perses informed that he will get it in few minutes.

Urases stood up, looked at the gathering and spoke, "Salutations. I welcome each one of you. Perses and his friends have done a wonderful work for this gathering. I am happy to see each of you enjoying. Glarton has finished all his training within 3 years." The crowd started clapping and praised, "Great, Great." Urases lifted his hand to calm them.

He continued, "Glarton is an honest, and hardworking pupil. Many of us will be worried that he is leaving. Do not worry because he is coming back to Coven and planned to become more familiar in future." Saying these Urases glanced at Rhea and Glarton. Glarton looked at everybody, lifted his hands, joined them together and moved it around, a gesture to show that he is happy about it. Whereas Rhea, who was feeling shy, did not know how to react, hence she looked down.

The crowd looked confused, and started talking about it. Few understood what the master meant and was surprised and wished long life for them. Urases again lifted his hand to calm the crowd. "Now, all of you eat and enjoy this gathering and my blessings will always be there for Glarton." Urases walked into the building.

Once Urases left, musicians played music and almost all of them began dancing and shouting. Few were wishing the couple and asked them to join others in the dance. The couple started dancing. Glarton was speechless looking at Rhea, and she was blushing. While dancing, he tried to hold her hand to pull her close to him. Because of the crowd, she smiled and moved away. In their custom, only after marriage, a man and woman can hold hands or stand close to each other in a gathering. Glarton understood her situation. He felt his pouch to ensure the gift is still there.

Glarton spoke in a low voice, "Ho Rhea! you look like a celestial. Your beauty is indescribable." He looked at her and filled his eyes with her face. She could not take her eyes off him. When she saw Perses coming close to them, she moved away. Perses was carrying a plate having three glasses of wine. He signaled Glarton and Rhea to come near a table.

The three sat around the table and drank their wine. They were talking about the interesting incidents that happened in the last three years and were laughing aloud. Perses went to the kitchen where Ereblan gave him two ceramic dishes. Perses kept them on the table in front of Glarton, and Rhea and said, "Glarton, this is the sweet I told you about." Saying this Perses handed one bowl to Glarton and other to Rhea.

Glarton asked, "Are you not going to eat the sweet?"

"I will eat later."

"Why later. Go, get your bowl and eat with us." Perses went back inside to get a bowl of sweet for him.

Glarton was about to eat the sweet from his bowl, Rhea stopped him and said, "Glarton, since Perses has made this sweet, let me eat first and then recommend." She ate a little from her bowl and said, "It is good!"

"My dear, it is tasting good because you tasted it. Let me also eat from your bowl." He started eating from her bowl. Rheas saw Perses coming out with his bowl of sweet. She got tensed and moved her bowl to Glarton and took his bowl and started eating.

Glarton said, "Perses, it smells and tastes good. Did you cook it?"

"Yes, I did."

Rhea giggled and asked in surprise, "Did you?"

"Yes, Rhea. I did."

"I never knew that you can cook food!" Saying this she laughed. Perses sat next to Rhea and ate along with them.

The gathering was almost over. It was getting late. Glarton wanted to give Rhea the gift, which he mentioned at the waterfalls. They went to Rheas' room in the center building. They went near the window, where their love began. Both looked outside the window, then exchanged looks and laughed. Glarton sat on a chair and pulled Rhea to sit on his lap. Holding Rheas' hand, Glarton told, "My soul, my life, Rhea, I love you. I want to begin a wonderful life with you."

Holding Glartons' face, Rhea said, "I want to spend the rest of my life with you. I will be counting every day, and every night till you come back to me."

Glarton hugged her gently and landed his lips on hers. While his lips gently touched hers, he could feel her body getting warm. He took the stone from the pouch and showed it to her. "Hope you like my gift." She looked at it, "Ho Glarton, this is wonderful. Where you found this stone?" Rhea took it from Glartons' hand. The center blue core of the stone opened up, filled the surrounding transparent stone and it fully turned to a blue color stone.

Rhea exclaimed, "Great. It also changes color!"

"What? No, it does not. But, it does change to blue when the person holding it..,"

He at once grabbed it from her hand and opened his hand. The stone gradually changed to its original form. Glarton placed the stone in the other hand of Rhea. It again completely became a blue color stone. He gazed at Rhea and screamed, "Ho no!, no, no!"

Rhea asked, "Glarton, what happened?"

"Rhea, are you feeling good? Are you having any pain or difficulty?" Rhea was wondering why was he asking these. Holding his hand she asked, "Why are you restless? What is going on with the stone changing color?" In the next moment, she glided to the floor. Blood was oozing out of her nose and mouth.

Glarton shouted, "Rhea, Rhea." He carried her, and shouted harder, "Help! I Need help." Nobody was there. Screaming "Aaayyy…, somebody come," he ran to the stairs.

Carrying Rhea, he came down the stairs, and kept shouting for help. Hearing this, few who were still in the gathering, entered the building. They were shocked to see Glarton carrying Rhea in his arms, who was senseless. Urases, who was in his office, heard the screaming. He came out and saw Glarton carrying Rhea and gasped, "Glarton, what happened? Why are you shouting, and Rhea…," he saw blood drooling from Rheas' mouth and nose; "Rhea! My dear, what happened?"

Glarton laid her down at the entrance, with her head on his lap.

Urases was shivering and found difficulty to approach her. He asked, "Glarton, what happened to my daughter?"

"Rhea is poisoned."

"What?... but how?" He stood there frozen.

Glarton seeing Urases frozen, he began shaking his masters' hand, "Sir, do something." Urases kneeled down next to Rhea and holding her hand, he called, "Rhea, Rhea, can you hear me?" Looking at Rheas' arm, which was slowly turning pale and blue he stopped calling. He patted her on both cheeks, no response, then shook her face side to side. Unfortunately, there was no response from Rhea. She laid there still with blood continuously oozing from her mouth, nose and her whole-body slowly turning blue and cold.

Urases examined her wrist for pulse. There was no reaction from him, only tears kept running down his cheeks. Glarton looked at Urases, who could not put words in his mouth. He struggled and mumbled few words, "She left us." Glarton seemed not to understand and looked confused. With teary eyes, Urases declared, "She passed away." Glarton lifted her head brought it close to his chest and hugged it gently. He could not control his emotion; he shook her body with a shriek, "Rheaaaahh!"

The stone from her hand rolled over and stopped beside Urasess' feet. The blue color vanished and it gradually turned to its normal color.

CHAPTER 19

GLARTON, A MURDERER

"This is going to be the happiest day of my life. Thenceforth, Glarton will no longer come in between me and Rhea. In few moments, Glarton will be dead. Rhea will be sad for few days, thenceforth, I will slowly get closer to her heart and finally she will forget him and marry me." As Perses was saying this to Ereblan at the cook house, his eyes were twinkling and he was feeling thirsty. He went to the water bucket and using the wood cup he gulped some water. He wanted to continue his sentence, but was feeling hot flushes on his face. So, he splashed cold water on his face. "Ereblan, …. My friend… I am not feeling well."

He sensed something chill coming out of his nose, he touched it and shocked to see blood oozing from his nose. "What is happening to me?"

Ereblan was still and in deep thought.

Perses yelled, "Are you listening to me?"

There were noises heard outside; men were shouting, "What happened? Call the physician."

Ereblan smiled and said, "Do n-n-not worry Perses, Glarton will accompany you."

"What do you mean by that?" Perses continued in a deep painful voice, "Why blood is dripping from my nose?"

"My apology, Perses. I actually mixed the poison n-n-not in one but two bowls."

"What? But why?"

"Perses, you told me to mix the poison in one of the two bowls, which you carried out first. But the truth is I wanted to mix poison in both, s-s-since Glarton has to die. Without a doubt I kn-n-now that you will n-n-not allow me to poison Rheas' dish; you are foolishly in love with her. Hence, I poured poison in only one bowl."

Perses was listening with blood oozing from his mouth.

Ereblan continued, "Glarton s-s-shall n-n-not be allowed to escape from death and at any cost nobody should know I did. But since Glarton is a prince, you may get caught and what if you point your finger at me. So, I had no choice but to mix poison in your bowl too."

Perses exhaled heavily and said, "Glarton has to die, he should."

Perses asked, "Why?"

"Ho Perses! A long story…. I do n-n-n-ot think you have enough time left to listen." He saw Perses glide down on the floor dead.

Being the father, Urases badly wanted to know how is daughter was killed and by who. But he has lost all his energy seeing Rhea dead.

He was sitting on the steps and at slightly above level Glarton on the floor. Glarton held Rheas' limp body from behind and supported her head on his left arm. Both Urases and Glarton were in shock. The physician was examining Rhea and trying to give medicinal herbs. Rheas' aunt came running and stood in front of them. Sitting down next to Rhea, she screamed and cried, called her name aloud and tried to wake her up. These crying and screaming, gathered more people around that place. With a heavy heart, the physician confirmed her death. He informed Urases that the death could be because of poison.

At the same time, a student came yelling, "Sir Urases, come to the literature building! Perses is lying on the floor with blood oozing from his nose and mouth!" Immediately, students standing near the entrance ran inside. Perses' mother ran, followed by Urases and the physician. They saw Perses lying on the floor in the passage. Perses' mother sat beside him took his head and kept on her lap and wailed, "Oh! Perses, my dear son, wake up. What happened to you?" The physician examined him, and declared that he is dead. Moreover, he mentioned that he is also been poisoned in a similar manner.

The physician rushed out of the building, looked at Glarton and yelled pointing towards the left side building, "Perses is dead! He too was poisoned." He then turned to the crowd and shouted, "All of you, listen. Does any of you have any pain or feeling uneasy? Come to me without delay." First, the crowd was confused, but after sometime they understood that he is suspecting the feast could have been poisoned. The people in the crowd looked at each other, and spoke to each other to confirm they were safe.

One of the students asked, "What did the poison do?"

The physician replied, "It will slowly react by affecting every part of the body one after another. The whole body will change to blue color. This poison can be mixed with the food and the person eating cannot find any difference in flavor, color or taste."

Hearing this Glarton said, "The dish! The sweet." He looked at Urases, who seemed to be confused. Glarton mentioned about the special dish, which Perses cooked for him and served him and Rhea. Urases called the worker in charge of the feast and inquired about the special dish. He agreed that Perses and Ereblan were preparing the dish, specially made for Glarton and Rhea. Glarton placed Rhea gently on the floor and ran to the cook house like a mad man in search of Ereblan. He searched all over the building, then found him at the forepart of the center building debating with someone.

"Ereblan!" yelled Glarton.

Ereblan was perplexed. Glarton yelled again, "Ereblan! What did you do?"

"What did I do?" asked Ereblan.

"The sweet that you and Perses cooked, it has killed Rhea. Why did you add poison?"

"I added n-n-nothing. I helped Perses in cooking, and after cooking I left the place. I do n-n-not kn-n-now what happened then."

Glarton jumped on Ereblan, pushed him to the floor and gripping his nape whispered in the ears, "Ereblan, you know everything. Tell me what happened?" Tightening his grip, Glarton added, "I will not hold back to chop your neck into pieces."

Ereblan was not willing to abide. He pushed Glarton away and yelled, "You may be the prince of a kingdom, but you cannot blame me like this." Glarton was full of rage. He raised his hand to attack Ereblan again but Urases stopped him and requested him to be with Rhea.

Meanwhile the sun commenced its work of rising in the east. It was cloudy, as if the climate is feeling sad because of the demise. Elderly people who were present there started to make arrangements for the rituals.

Glarton sat close to Rhea, who was lying on a bed made of plantain leaves. Glarton heart still refused to accept the fact. He hoped that she is only sleeping, and will wake up at any moment. Perses body was placed adjacent to hers, on a bed made of coconut leaves. The sun has risen well above the river, to see what is going on here. The elders and surrounding people tried to talk to Urases hoping that he will get some solace. He had good reputation, but what so ever, his life is forever shattered and everyone is aware how much he was fond of his daughter. Seeing this one of the elders comforted Urases saying, "Do not do this to you. I understand it is deeply sad but it is the fate of your daughter and nobody can stop it."

"No, it is not a fate," a student yelled from the group. He added, "It is not a fate. Master could have stopped it." Urases could not understand why the student is yelling like this. The elder asked the student the reason for him to say like that. The pupil replied, "We are aware that Perses loved Rhea and she also liked him."

Urases screamed, "What foolish talk is going on here?"

Ereblan spoke, "S-s-sir, it is n-n-not foolish but a truth, which n-n-needs to be brought to everyone's attention."

"What are you saying Ereblan?"

"S-s-sir, as a close friend of Perses, I kn-n-new that they both were willing to get married, but they n-n-never mentioned it to you. As Glarton un-n-nderstood this, he approached you and told his wish to marry Rhea. Maybe you agreed to Glarton: because he is a Prince with power and wealth."

One of the teachers added, "What he says might be true. In the gathering, when the master indirectly declared about Glarton and Rhea, only Glarton was happy, but Rhea was not happy. She was quiet and looking down."

"Yes, s-s-she kept quiet: s-s-she got carried away with wealth and power which speaks more than love."

Urases wanted to strongly rebuke Ereblan and the others but the present situation is not appropriate so he kept quiet. But Glarton could not keep quiet, after listening Ereblan slander Rhea; he stood up and shouted with rage, "Ereblan, how could you talk like that about Rhea? You are not aware of the truth. You cannot foretell the true thoughts of someone only by the action they did or not. Rhea is a pure soul. She truly loved me. Do not ever talk ill about her."

There were voices of altercations in the crowd. An elder stepped forward and ordered the crowd to keep peace and disperse. Glarton went inside the center building. Urases followed Glarton, who went to Rheas' study. Glarton was sitting next to the window where he saw her first. He was weeping, holding stone in one hand and Rheas' pearl necklace in another. On seeing Urases entering, he wiped off his tears.

Urases spoke, "Glarton."

"Rhea truly loved me. She never had any feelings towards Perses. It shreds my heart hearing those ill talk about my Rhea," said Glarton with tear laden eyes.

Urases looked outside through the window and sobbed, "Rhea, you are not fortunate to lead a life with this wonderful person, who truly loves you." He wiped off his tears and spoke, "Glarton, whatever is the situation do not forget who you are; a Prince, a hope for many people. You were sent here chiefly for the training, which is done. You have an obligation, a kingdom to rule. You have to forget all these bad incidents and return to Azunt for a prosperous future. Why do you have to delay your journey back?"

Glarton cannot discern. Urases exhaled heavily, "I do not know how to bring this forth." He turned away from Glarton and with a heavy voice he said, "Do not be aggrieved, depart immediately."

"What? But why?" Urases was finding it difficult to explain him. After a pause, in a firm voice Glarton said, "I will not. I shall find the murderer and tear him into pieces and thenceforth I will depart this land."

"Glarton, can you not see what is happening here? I knew that Perses liked Rhea. He could not accept that you and Rhea were in love. He also warned me on what you both were doing is wrong. He was upset and angry with me. I expected he will create a rift between you and Rhea. But I never imagined… cha," he thumped his fist with a loud thud and said, "That beast, distrustful Perses will go to this extent to kill my dear daughter."

Glarton screamed, "No, Perses will not kill Rhea or kill himself. He was determined to live with Rhea. He will kill me but not Rhea."

"By killing you, the prince, he will get in to deep trouble. Moreover, he could not have won Rheas' heart," said Urases. "He is a coward, who killed himself and ensured you do not get Rhea. Glarton, I want my daughter to receive her final rituals without any unpleasantness. She is being slandered even after her death. This is crueller. I…," Urases could no longer stand, he sat on the floor and sobbed, "My precious is gone, but her death rituals should take place properly. We believe that if it is not completed peacefully, the soul does not rest in peace. Therefore, you have to…".

Glarton spoke earnestly, "Sir, I beg you to allow me to be here for at least today. I still feel her presence here."

"I understand your emotions, can you not understand mine?"

"I have to find the murderer. I will chop him little by little into pieces and quench my vengeance," screamed Glarton.

Urases wiped his tears, stood up and spoke in a firm voice, "I am not only requesting this as a father, but also as your teacher. Go away from this place."

Glarton became speechless; his throat was choking with emotions. He bowed to Urases and said, "Sir, I thank you for the teaching. "Salutations Sir." Without any delay, he went to his room and began his journey back to Azunt.

CHAPTER 20

THE ARROW STRIKE

In the sky, the setting sun was giving out a sad glow: it was unhappy with the situation. Glarton took his things and left his room and the building. Some understood his feelings, and did not want to bother him. Most thought that Glarton is the villain, who was responsible for Rhea and Perses committing suicide.

As Glarton was walking, he could hear people passing bad comments. He neither responded nor stopped but kept walking quietly. His lips were sealed but his heart was bleeding with the pain of loss and his thoughts were fuming with the inability to reap vengeance. When he reached the spot where he saw Rhea for the first time in his life; he stopped, lifted his head and saw the same window. Rhea was standing there with her eyes full of tears and her lips repeating "Do not go... do not go." Tears rolled down on Glartons' face. With a heavy heart he continued walking.

Camigo, King Themtons' friend, who has come to a nearby town for trading, heard regarding the death of Sir Urases' daughter. He at once reached the University. After reaching, he found out what happened there and Glarton had been blamed. When he asked for Glarton, many hesitated to say anything. One of the maids told that Glarton left the place few hours earlier and was heading towards North. Camigo was worried; he guessed that Glarton could have gone towards the Coven Gate. He stroked his horse with spur to reach Coven Gate.

Near the border of Zeulean and Lumbian community Glarton was riding on his horse which trotted through the twilight. He was thinking about the three beautiful years he has spent with Rhea: her eyes, her smile, and her innocence. Every time they met; he saw her eyes pouring love for him. They dreamt about the future together: going to different places in Azunt, bearing their children, and serving the people. Ho no! I cannot live without her.

Why should I return? Even if I go back and take care of the kingdom, there will be emptiness in my soul. Can I bring peace to my soul? Why Perses, why? Is it possible that he has done it? No... no... He would kill me, but not kill Rhea or himself. Whoever killed my Rhea, why did you spare me? You rascal! You should have killed me too. You gave me the horrible punishment, of being alive without my Rhea. I will find you. For certain, I will. Then I will give you the worst punishment that you will beg that you should not have born in this world. While these thoughts kept wavering in his mind, he was neither aware of the path nor direction. The horse could sense his masters' pain, so without bothering him, it kept trotting in the direction having a clear path.

Upon reaching the foot hills of Mount Agua, a searing heat pierced his heart. He pressed his chest and dismounted the horse. "Glarton! Glarton…," he heard somebody desperately calling out his name. He turned back, but nobody was there. But in the far distance, he saw smoke. In Coven, they believed that when a young unmarried woman dies, her soul becomes a heavenly individual. So, the corpse must be respected by carrying it to the nearby mountain top and after ritual it should be burnt. Glarton realized that they have taken Rhea to the top of the mountain and burnt her body; he lost his strength. He could no longer stand, and fell down on the ground.

After laying there for a long time, he heard hoofsteps approaching towards him. He could vaguely see a man dismount; approaching him by calling his name. He splashed water on Glartons' face, lifted his head and poured little water in his mouth. Glarton opened his eyes and saw Camigo.

Camigo asked, "Prince Glarton, what happened?"

Glarton did not reply; he looked at Camigo and seemed lost.

Camigo tapped Glartons' cheek and said, "Glarton… Glarton?"

In a feeble voice Glarton replied, "Yes."

"You are weak so, kindly come with me. You can take rest and tomorrow allow me to take you to Coven Gate."

Glarton agreed and followed Camigo. They reached Camigos' home. Camigo offered food, but Glarton did not eat anything. Since Camigo kept requesting, he ate little and went to rest. His body was tired, but his thoughts were wide awake. His eyes told him that he is at Camigos' home, but his heart gave an illusion of him sitting on the steps at the Madiantes with Rheas' face on his lap saying, 'Glarton, my love, my life, come back soon and marry me.' Glarton sat up and screamed, "I will marry you, Rhea! I will. Wake up, I cannot live without you." Camigo heard Glartons' screaming, and sobbing sound. He can understand his pain. Glarton fell asleep after crying for a while.

Glarton woke up early in the morning. The first thought came to his mind was, 'I have to go back. Go back now to Madiantes and find the swine who took away the love of my life and cut every part of his body slowly till his last breath.' He could no longer stop himself from going back to Madiantes. Not informing Camigo, he galloped his horse towards the south. He was few miles away from Camigos' house, where suddenly he heard a 'Hooosh' sound. Before he could turn to the direction of the sound, an arrow was approaching him from the left. The arrow lacerated a small part of his chest and he fell down to the ground. The sharp pain caused him to scream, "Aahh!"

Blood was oozing from his chest. As he was mentally and physically tired, he could not react fast. Slowly he stood up, looked around, saw nobody but a horse coming towards him. He removed his sword from the scabbard, which was hanging on his horse. Collecting his remaining strength, he stood steady to fight. But before the horse could reach him, he sensed another arrow from behind. Glarton sat down on the ground and saw the rider on the horse shooting arrow.

As the horse kept nearing him, Glarton realized Camigo was riding the horse, who kept shooting arrows far behind Glarton. They could hear the enemy riding away from them. Camigo dismounted from his horse. Glartons' strength gave up; he fell on Camigo. Camigo laid Glarton on the floor. He took the toga, which he carried in his horse, and tied it around Glartons' chest and underarms to stop the bleeding.

"Glarton! Glarton! Can you hear me?" There was no answer. He gently put Glarton on his horse and with a rope tied the halter of Glartons' horse to his horse. He rode faster ensuring nobody was following. Glarton was in such a condition that he did not realize his ride to Camigos' home, or the physicians' face, or the stitches he got on his right chest.

Camigo sent message to King Themton. He mentioned that he will come along with Glarton till Goptm Cape and requested King Themton to send someone to receive Prince Glarton. Glarton woke up after two days. He felt pain on his right chest. He touched it and saw a cloth wrapped around his left shoulder and right underarm. Camigo was glad seeing Glarton awake. He inquired about his health.

"What happened?" asked Glarton. Camigo explained the incident.

"I remember something like an arrow from the side, fast and accurate, to pierce my heart. It scratched my chest," said Glarton in a feeble voice.

"Who could have done that?" asked Camigo. Glarton did not reply.

Camigo continued, "The physician told me that the arrow tip had poison. If the arrow had lacerated deep, you could have died in few moments and nothing can be done to save you."

'Poison! Immediate death?' Glarton repeated these in his mind.

"Glarton, you need rest. Do not try to go to Madiantes again. That day I was able to follow you and save you. But this may not be possible again. Kindly listen, it is safer to return to Azunt without any further delay."

Next day morning Glarton was feeling better. He could move his right arm, and shoulder without much pain. They started their journey. Camigo told, "We need to be careful and vigilant on our way to the Gate."

"Uncle, are you certain that there was only one person who tried to kill me?"

"When I was nearing the place, I saw you holding your right chest and falling down. I yelled by your name. To your left side, at a far distance, I saw a person approaching you. I started shooting arrow at him. He tried to shoot another arrow; on hearing my voice, and me shooting arrow, he stepped back and ran away."

Glarton questioned, "Is there a possibility of his group hiding behind the trees and only he came forward to see if I am dead?"

"Yes, possible! But when I was carrying you, if there were others, they could have easily attacked me. Also, I heard only a pair of footsteps running in to the woods."

"Hmm… Who could it be?"

Camigo questioned, "Could it be someone from the academy?" Glarton gave a surprised look. "I mean, since they have a false impression on you, one of the well-wishers of Urases or Perses could have attacked you."

Glarton replied, "I thought the same. On the contrary, why they have to wait till I reach the foot of the mountain? They could have attacked soon after I left Madiantes. The person who followed me is highly trained in silent movements. I could not hear anything."

"Let us move fast. I have asked some men, whom I know, to accompany us till the Cape of Goptm."

"No uncle, let me go alone."

"Alone! It is not safe."

Looking straight into Camigos' eyes, Glarton said "Alone, I will meet the person trying to kill me. I will not allow another soul to be hurt on my behalf. If he is determined to kill me, seeing me going back alone, he will attack."

Camigo insisted, "I understand Prince, still let me come with you. Do not deny this. I am not only your fathers' friend, but also responsible for you and the trust your father has on me."

CHAPTER 21

THE MISSING FINGERS

Glarton and Camigo reached the Coven Gate. During the entire journey, Camigo kept looking around, ensuring nobody was following or attacking. Inspite of Glarton disapproval, Camigo arranged few of his men to follow them at a far distance.

Glarton requested, "Shall we meet mother Maurea, before getting onto the boat."

Camigo was not approval of this, "Prince, may I ask, is there any particular reason? I feel the earlier we leave the safer it will be."

In a heavy voice Glarton replied, "I want to return the stone."

Camigo empathized and nodded his head. Glarton went to the chief guard and introduced himself. The chief guard was happy to see him again.

Glarton requested, "I wish to meet Mother Maurea. Kindly inform her."

Chief guard said, "I will be more than happy to do that. Unfortunately, she will not be seeing anyone."

"May I ask the reason?"

"She is ill."

"What happened?" asked Glarton.

"Ten days ago, two men arrived at the Coven Gate. The guards brought them to me. One was tall and other was short. They introduced themselves as fugitives from the North. When I enquired, they told there was severe drought due to which many people died. Carrying remaining food, these two men left their town in a boat along with four other men." The Chief stopped and ordered to bring some hot tea for them.

Sipping the tea, the Chief proceeded, "After two days of sailing they realized that they were lost in the sea. On the third day, food and water were depleted. On the fourth day, the men were starving and dying of thirst. One of the men drank too much of sea water and got sick. He vomited many times and at last he fainted. The tall man told that they had no choice except to throw him in the water. Looking at the horrible situation of hunger and thirst, one of the men fell into the water and committed suicide."

As the Chief was talking, Camigo started to lose interest. For him, Prince reaching Goptm was important and any other action was only wasting time. Chief continued, "On the fourth night, they saw light from this land. So, with whatever strength they had, they sailed the boat towards this land. As the boat was approaching the land, it hit a rock and broke into pieces and the men started swimming towards the land. As they were already weak, the heavy current of the water in the night made it difficult for them to swim. Only these two men were able to reach the shore. They do not know what happened to the other two men. They might have drowned in the water."

"Ho! It is sad. Glad that two men were able to reach," said Glarton

"Prince, I am not happy about that," said Chief. Glarton and Camigo gave a perplexed look. Chief continued, "On listening to their story, we felt bad and provided food and shelter to them. Initially, they behaved well and did all the chores assigned to them. They were calm and quiet; nobody even felt their presence. On the third day, from morning till the noon the guard saw the tall man working outside the hut whereas the short one did not come out. When the guard enquired the tall man, he informed that he is not familiar but suspected the missing short man may be a spy. Immediately, I sent men to search for the short man all over the Coven Gate."

"After few minutes of searching, the guards found the short person. They brought him to me. I asked him in a gentle tone, he refused to open his mouth. I asked him with a stern voice, and then yelled at him. Even then, he did not open his mouth. I had no choice except to torture him. The information he revealed was shocking. Both are trained killers. The purpose of their journey to Coven was to kill someone. The tall man, who was in the hut, was responsible to deliver the most poisonous material to a man living in the south of Coven."

When the chief guard said this both Camigo and Glarton were frozen. Glarton whispered in Camigos' ears, "An aimed conspiracy to murder."

Camigo nodded his head, at the same time gestured Glarton not to say anything more in front of the Chief. Seeing Glarton whisper, the Chief stopped and asked them what it was?

Glarton asked, "Did the short man mention the name of the person?"

"No, he was not alive to say anything else."

Camigo asked, "Not alive?"

"When the guards brought him to me, his hands were well tied behind. When he spoke about the poison, he began to cough and requested us for water. I let the guards untie him to drink water. His right-hand and wrist was wrapped with a cloth Suddenly, he tore the cloth with his teeth and inside was a pellet like thing. He swallowed the pellet and then blood started oozing out through his nose and mouth. His body turned blue and died."

"When the guards examined his wrist, we found that his right hand had only two fingers. It seems that the other fingers were cut using a sword. I realized their conspiracy. When we were behind the short man, the tall man escaped Coven Gate to deliver the poison. When we ran back to the hut, it was late and the tall person has escaped. I ordered the guards to search for him, but could not find him." The chief guard looked down in disappointment.

Camigo said, "Then!"

"I informed Mother Maurea about the incidents. She was worried, and she predicted worst will happen. Three days ago, we got the news that Sir Urases' daughter Rhea and her cousin was poisoned and they died. She felt guilty for what happened. Thenceforth, she did not eat or sleep." He frowned, "Prince, if I am not wrong you are coming from south. Do you know what happened?"

Glarton could not say anything. His emotions were choking his throat. Camigo understood and he responded to the chief guard, "It is a heart-breaking loss. They are in deep sorrow. Chief, it is time for us to leave. We need to get on the boat to Cape of Goptm.

In a weak voice Glarton asked, "Can you guess where he could have gone?"

Chief Guard asked, "You mean the tall man?"

"Yes."

"Unfortunately, I do not know."

"Chief, I have to meet Mother. I will be careful not to talk anything, except to give her something!"

"My apologies Prince. She is not willing to meet anyone for now. I can pass it to her on your behalf."

Glarton took the stone from his pouch and handed it to the Chief. With the stone in his hand the guard queried, "Is this the stone which was given to you as a gift from Mother?"

"Yes, it is."

"May I ask, why you want to return the stone? She may not feel good about it."

Glarton replied, "It is a huge burden to me. Can you give this to her and convey that the purpose of the stone is fulfilled!"

Glarton and Camigo started walking towards the wharf. The boat was floating on the water like a lotus leaf. Glarton was in deep thought.

Camigo advised, "Do not feel bad son. Life has to move on."

"I am not feeling bad. I feel anger." Glarton tightened his fists and remarked, "One thing is clear Uncle, a big conspiracy: to kill Rhea, Perses, and now me. It is possible that the tall man who delivered the poison to Perses, is trying to kill me."

"For what?"

"I do not have the answer for it, but in the next opportunity I will not leave him alive."

CHAPTER 22

CATASTROPHE

Camigo and Glarton got on to Theoi Halioi, the boat which is used for transporting people from coven to Goptm and other way. As the boat started, the sun started setting in the west. After few minutes, the sky was quickly accumulating thick clouds for no reason and these clouds were hindering the setting sun rays. The blurred light from the oil lantern lamps were providing a vague view. Camigo and Glarton sat in one of the cabins. Looking at Glarton, Camigo said, "Prince, since we have left Mother Maureas' hut, you are quiet and worried. It is bothering me seeing you like this."

With a heavy sigh, Glarton responded, "When I left Azunt, I felt that someone was following me to the Goptm. Then during my stay at the Hut, one of the workers suspected that the person in the adjacent hut could be a spy." He glimpsed at the waves and then turned to Camigo, "When I was at Madiantes, few times I felt like being watched. Rhea poisoned and now someone trying to kill me. It is certain that trained killers were sent to deliver the poison. There must be some connection in all these incidents but I am not able to think clearly."

Camigo touched Glartons' shoulder and spoke in a soft voice, "Glarton, you are tired: both mentally and physically. It will take some time to reach Cape, meanwhile take some rest. I will wake you." Glarton agreed.

Camigo went to the deck. After a short while, the clouds became thicker and started raining with heavy wind. The sea waves started to toss and the surging tides were rolling the boat. People at the deck were getting worried. Glarton woke up because of the toss and yaw. He tried to arise; suddenly he felt a heavy blow. Someone hit him on his head from behind. He suspected it could be the killer. He was not able to stand due to the pain in his head. He was determined to see the person who was trying to kill him so, he pretended to be unconscious.

The killer slowly approached Glarton, who slowly removed the sword from his scabbard. The killer came near Glarton, took his long thin sword in his right hand and aimed to cut Glartons' neck. As he moved the sword, 'Clung' Glarton defended killers' sword with his.

Not expecting this move from Glarton, the killer stood shocked for a moment. He instantly swung his sword with a heavy force. Glarton used his complete strength to defend it. He swung his sword with a heavy force, at the same time kicking the killer on his chest with a heavy push. The killer dropped his sword on one side and fell off on the other side. Immediately, the killer stood up to run away, but Glarton grabbed his neck from behind and pushed him on the floor.

Glarton jumped on the killer who rolled to right side. Glarton clutched the shoulder of the killer from behind and was trying to remove the black mask which was covering the face. The killer resisted him from removing the mask. Glarton noticed there were only 3 fingers in his left hand. This reminded of the two men the Chief guard was mentioning about.

"Who are you? Which kingdom you belong to?" asked Glarton. The killer did not answer and kept twisting and bending his body to get rid of Glartons' grip. His body was flexible; he slipped out of Glartons' hold.

At the same time on the deck people were shouting seeing the formation of a whirlpool. With passing moment, the whirlpool was engulfing its surroundings. The boat was getting dragged towards the sea monster. The sailors were trying hard to sail the boat away from it. The heavy wind and high currents were making it difficult. The chief sailor climbed up the sail stick and removed the long white cloth, which was pulling the boat more towards its lover. The boat was swaying and pitching towards the whirlpool, as if it was ready to end its life. Few were screaming for help and few were running helter-skelter. Some jumped into the water hoping to save their lives and some used the barrel from the boat to swim.

Inside the cabin, neither Glarton nor the killer wanted to give up their fight. At one point they reached the edge; Glarton pushed him over the edge. The killer headed outside and due to the swaying of the boat, he fell on the edge of the boat. Now both realized the situation outside. Holding the edge with one hand killer turned his body and with his right leg gave a heavy blow on Glartons' head.

Since Glarton already had a wound on the head, the second one gave him severe pain and it was muddied with blood. Supporting his head with both the hands, he kneeled down. Using this situation, the killer searched for something sharp around. There was a long metal stick at the edge of the boat, which was holding the flag. The killer tried to pull it out of the boat rim. He almost got it.

The inward pulling of the boat by the whirlpool, and the outward sailing of the boat, gave the boat a big jerk. Because of this the killer lost his balance and fell on the metal rod, which he was trying to pluck. It pierced his stomach, and came out on the other side. "Aaghhh!" shrieked the killer. He looked at Glarton and then at his left hand with missing fingers. This reminded killer of the day his fingers were chopped because he was not loyal to his master. The bad memory brought him agony, he roared loud like a lion and pulled the metal rod out of his stomach.

Hearing the scream, Glarton, for one last time, gathered his strength and ran towards the killer. He suspected that the killer would kill him with the rod, so he booted the pierced stomach of the killer. It created heavy pain for the killer and he dropped the rod. The killer realized that the best thing to do is to escape from there. He tried to jump into the water. Glarton leaned forward and caught the falling killer. Glartons' one hand was gripping killers' arm and shoulder and other hand tried to pull down the mask.

"Ereblan!?" yelled Glarton.

Ereblan kept twisting his body to get rid of Glartons' hold. Glarton asked again "Ereblan? You... Were you the one trying to kill me?"

"Haa... Haa..." smiled Ereblan. The pain on his stomach and his inability to kill Glarton made Ereblan angrier. He shouted with despair, "Yes, it is me!"

Glarton pulled him up, held his robe, and started thrashing him without restraint. When he saw Ereblans' limbs were giving away and about to faint, he dragged him close to his eyes and asked, "Were you the one following me from Azunt?"

Ereblan tried to slide away from Glartons' hold, but he could not as he was feeling weak. He denied, "No, I was not following you from Azunt."

"Were you the one staying in the hut and spying over me?"

Ereblan exclaimed, "Do you think I am the only one who wants to kill you?"

"What are you saying?"

"You will understand soon!"

"I thought you were a close friend of Perses. Did he ask you to kill me?"

"Ho! He does not have that much courage."

"Then, why? Why you wanted to see me dead?"

Ereblan did not respond except kept smiling. Glarton pushed Ereblan down on the floor and gave a heavy kick on his stomach. Ereblan screamed of pain. "Ereblan you must disclose the truth right away. Why?" demanded Glarton. Ereblan did not respond but curled up into a ball, holding his stomach in agony.

"You malicious swine! Tell me."

Ereblan still kept quiet. Glarton pressed his foot against Ereblans' stomach and pulled his head back by holding his hair. He took the rod and pointed it on the neck of Ereblan and said "You speak now, or you will be beheaded."

Ereblan opened his mouth, "I entered Coven as a common man, became friend with Perses by saving him, when I myself arranged for the snake to kill him. At Madiantes, few times I tried to kill you, but you escaped. Urases began suspecting me, so I stopped to do it by myself. One day I found out about you and Rhea. I informed Perses and used it to create problem between you and Perses. Even during the Tournament, I was hoping a lot that Perses will kill you."

Ereblan grinded his teeth as he said, "But you saved his pride." With howl of anguish he yelled, "I cannot let you go back to Azunt. Glarton, the Prince of Azunt should not return back alive."

Glarton took a step back hearing this and wondered whether this is beyond what he suspected. Ereblan continued, "I sent message for my fellow men, who got me the most silent killing poison. I instigated Perses to kill you by adding poison in the sweet which Perses prepared for you. I was certain you will die so, I killed Perses by mixing poison in his bowl too. Unfortunately, you did not die rather Rhea ate and sacrificed her life for you" As Ereblan was saying this, tears of anger were flowing from Glartons' eyes.

"Then I created problem, so people will gather and kill you or punish you by their way of shredding your back with lashes until you die. Sad it did not happen and you left the place alone. Ensuring you are alone, I followed and at a good point, aimed an arrow on you, I thought you are dead." He stamped the floor with his palm, and clenching his teeth he shouted, "This… this, my last opportunity, even this I failed. How am I going to face my master? No! no, I will face my master. I will kill you," saying this he rolled towards Glarton and kicked his knee. Glarton jumped up and bent his knee and punched Ereblans' stomach with his knee.

Ereblan could not move much. Glarton asked, "Who is your master?" Ereblan was quiet.

Glarton continued, "You should have come face to face with me and killed me. Why did you kill my life, my Rhea?" Even for this Ereblan kept quiet. Glarton pulled

Ereblan close to him, fixed his eyes on him and said, "You do not know what Rhea meant to me. You could have killed me in the North Island. Why do you have to do it in Coven?" Ereblan saw angry tears rolling down from Glartons' eyes. With a stern voice Ereblan answered, "You have to ask this to your father, King Themton."

Glarton gave a heavy slap, which made Ereblan fall on the floor. He pulled Ereblans' face closer to him and with wide eyes he asked, "What? My father!

"Yes, your father, the great King Themton."

"Why should I ask my father?"

Ereblan was quiet.

"Ereblan, before I start to cut each part of your body till you die, tell me what my father has to do with this?"

Looking straight into Glarton eyes, Ereblan gave a firm reply, "Go ask your father, if you return back alive."

"My father has nothing to do with this."

"Ha..Ha..Ha.." loudly laughed Ereblan. "This prince does not know anything about his own father or his kingdom. Ignorant."

Glarton was enraged, "Do not blabber. Tell me who is your master?"

Ereblan kept laughing. This added more fuel to Glartons' burning heart, he wanted to tear Ereblans' laughing face. Holding Ereblans' neck with one hand, Glarton turned to search for something sharp. At the same time the sailors were roaring very fast to move the boat away from the wind and whirlpool. This made Glarton loose his balance and he fell on the floor.

Using this opportunity, Ereblan quickly jumped in to the river. As he was trying to jump, he turned to Glarton and screamed, **"Glarton, you are going to die soon. This is not an end; this is a beginning for your end."**

www.ingramcontent.com/pod-product-compliance
Lightning Source LLC
Chambersburg PA
CBHW021212130726
47988CB00002B/619